Evernight Publishing

www.evernightpublishing.com

Copyright© 2015

Sam Crescent

Editor: Karyn White

Cover Artist: Sour Cherry Designs

Jacket Design: Jay Aheer

ISBN: 978-1-77233-505-7

CONTROL

DEDICATION

I want to dedicate this book to my lovely editor Karyn White. You're amazing and always help me with my books to make them the best they can be. Thank you so much for all your hard work and support.

CONTROL

Trojans MC, 1

Sam Crescent

Copyright © 2014

Chapter One

Duke Bana, president of the Trojans MC, watched as Holly Crock leaned over the table serving his son. She leaned over just enough for him to get a good view of her large tits. Unlike the sweet-butts who belonged to the club, Holly's rack was natural. Holly was no sweet-butt either. The whole of the club was gathered outside of the clubhouse to celebrate the Fourth of July. The old ladies had all cooked; the sweet-butts were on their best behavior, and they were all surrounded by their kids. His son, Matthew, was fourteen years old, and a little terror when he wanted to be, just like his old man. Glancing across the garden he saw Matthew's mother, his ex-wife, flirting outrageously with Pike, his vice president. From the look on Pike's face, he was embarrassed and irritated by the woman. Julie didn't have a clue that the club was disgusted by her. She fucked anything that would have her. Duke couldn't believe he'd married the bitch or fucked her, but then he looked at his son, and knew he'd not change a thing. He loved his little boy, who wasn't really little anymore. Matthew was growing up too fast. It wouldn't be long before he was prospecting for a place in the club.

Trojans MC was a hard-assed biker group. Duke had earned his place as president after Holly's father, Russ, had stepped down. He'd fought the men who demanded he prove himself, fucked the women they lined up for him, earning their respect and trust throughout the years he'd been part of the club. The Trojans was in his blood. Duke loved the club, the men, the whole life. He wouldn't change anything, but he would change Holly Crook's blatant disregard for him.

Grabbing his beer, he watched her as she moved down the line of kids, serving them each vegetables. She'd been one of those kids once. He remembered her growing up, spending a great deal of time at the club with Russ. She was close to her family and rarely went a week without visiting them, whether that be at the club or her parents' house. Duke had been at their home when she did visit. She never tried to pull him into small talk. In fact, she went out of her way to avoid him. Holly had gotten under his skin without even fucking trying.

She was twenty-one years old, way too young for him when he was thirty-nine. He shouldn't be interested in her, yet he couldn't stop watching her. Whenever she was in the room he perked up and not just his dick. She had long blonde hair. He spent too much time wondering what the silk strands would feel like wrapped around his fist as he plowed into her from behind. Duke loved his sex hot and dirty. Something in his gut told him Holly could be brought around to his way of having sex. When she did finally look at him, she had the brightest blue eyes he'd ever seen. They never gave anything away and could be mistaken for the dead cold of Antarctica. Holly didn't give anything of herself away. Duke had to work to get even a hello from her.

Her figure wasn't slender either. Holly had a nice big ass, large tits, and thighs that were thick, and big enough for man to hold onto. She was a full woman, completely the opposite of half of the sweet-butts. Julie, his ex-wife, was a slender woman with tits he'd bought as a present to himself. He had hated fucking Julie. She was so small and slender there were times he truly believed he'd been fucking a man. The tits were a gift just so he could get his rocks off.

"You've got to sort your bitch out. She really thinks she's something special," Pike said, taking a seat. "Also, if Russ sees your tongue hanging out for Holly, he'll kick your ass. He may not be president anymore, but no one touches his daughter."

Raoul, one of the other club brothers, had touched her. After he'd taken her virginity on prom night, Raoul had come back to the clubhouse to brag about his conquest. Out of all of the brothers, Raoul was the youngest at twenty-five years old. None of the brothers had appreciated his complete disrespect of Holly. They all took it in turns to teach him some respect, Russ included. Holly hadn't come around the club for a long while afterward and would always make excuses not to attend any club events. But Russ had talked to her, and she'd slowly started making an appearance once again. Duke had missed her, which made him realize how much he'd enjoyed merely seeing her. He never got anything else out of her.

Her presence had been missed, by him and also by the whole of the club.

Turning to look at Pike, Duke smiled. "I'm president now. It would be an honor for her to be my woman."

Pike spat his beer out laughing. They gained some attention from the brothers. Seeing Duke wasn't interested in any of them joining, none of the brothers made their way toward them.

Music filtered out of the clubhouse, which had been opened up for the event. A couple of the townspeople were among them. They were friends of the club and were always invited to participate.

"Fuck me, Duke. She's not like any of the other women here. Since Raoul fucked her over she's been more reserved than ever before. Also, I think she's seeing some guy in town."

Duke tensed, glancing toward Holly. He didn't make his attraction to her known. It was only Pike, his best friend, who knew anything about it. Pike had been there when he'd killed Julie's boyfriend. Three years ago Duke got a call from the school asking if he'd come and pick Matthew up. It had been past six, and the school hadn't been able to get in touch with anyone. The only numbers Matthew remembered were his home and the clubhouse number.

Pissed off, Duke had gotten Matthew and gone home only to find Julie in their bed, fucking the mailman. It had seen the end of the marriage, which had been a long time coming, the end of the mailman, and Julie out on her ass. She still came around the clubhouse, but he only allowed her because of Matthew.

"What do you know?"

"Nothing, but I now know for sure you're sniffing around Holly."

"You knew anyway," Duke said. He'd tried to hide his interest in the blonde beauty. She was younger than he was, but she had a heart of gold.

"No, I knew you thought she was pretty and wanted to fuck her. Wanting and actually having are two different things."

"I've not said I'm going to do anything about it," Duke said.

Pike laughed. "Yeah, you are."

He glanced across the compound toward Holly. She'd left the kids to eat and was talking to Mary, her friend who rarely visited the club. The last rumor Duke had heard was that Mary had a thing for Pike. Fuck, his club was turning into a school playground filled with gossip and rumors. He'd need to change it up.

"Whatever happens, Raoul isn't going near her." He wouldn't have that fucker hurting her again.

"It's your funeral when Russ gets near you. He's protective of his daughter."

Duke wasn't going to give Russ a chance to hurt him. He already had plans in motion, some the brothers didn't even know about.

****

"Duke's staring at you again," Mary said, putting the latest plate of cupcakes down on the stand.

Holly blew out a breath, pushing some of her blonde hair out of the way. She tugged all of her hair into a ponytail using the band she always kept on her wrist. "I'm going to need to get this cut soon."

"You've been saying that for the past year. Your mom has taken care of the split ends. You're never getting your hair cut." Mary tugged a strand that she'd missed.

"Get off." Holly swatted her hand away, laughing as Mary stuck her tongue out. They'd been best friends for a long time, since nursery. They had both stuck out like sore thumbs. Where the rest of the kids knew each other from other play groups or being neighbors, neither she nor Mary had been part of that. Holly had been a biker kid while Mary's parents were dirt poor. They stuck together throughout everything. Holly's father didn't mind Mary spending a lot of time with her. They stayed out of trouble and were the closest friends. Mary knew everything, including the disastrous night spent with Raoul.

"I see you're avoiding the point of Duke staring at you."

"You've been around gossip too long."

"Hey, I work at the diner. I can't exactly close my ears off. Everyone talks there."

Shaking her head, Holly picked up the tray of cupcakes. Each cake had a little flag out of the top. She and Mary had spent the whole day baking for the celebrations. "You're so fucking bad."

"Hey, you wouldn't guess, but Jessica, the bitch from high school, she's pregnant and it's not Nate's," Mary said, biting into a piece of carrot. Jessica and Nate, the cheerleader and the famous jock, were in the same year as they were in school.

"You're going to end up crazy listening to all that gossip. We've got to get you out of that diner." Holly carried the cupcakes over to the kids. Most of them had eaten the vegetables she'd asked them to. Their eyes lit up like the fireworks were going to at nightfall. When they'd all taken a cupcake, she took a breath and made her way over to the men, offering them each a cupcake.

Raoul stood with Bertie and Floss, talking and drinking.

"Cupcake," she asked, forcing herself to look at Raoul. She didn't have any feelings for the man other than revulsion. He thought he was some great stud, but to her, he was a complete and total asshole. Never judge a book by its cover, and she wouldn't judge any man by his looks ever again.

"Hey, baby. How are you doing?" Raoul asked.

She walked away without answering. He was worse than an asshole, a total bastard, maybe even worse. What kind of man fucked you, took your virginity, then went to the club and talked to everyone about? Her own father knew what they'd done before the weekend was over. He'd been so disappointed in her. Holly had seen the emotion in his eyes, and there was no getting away from it. It had been hard, and it was still hard to be around Raoul while her father was present. If she had a gun, she'd shoot the bastard.

Holly moved from each small gathering until she had no choice but to go to the main table where Duke and her father were sitting. She went to her father first.

"Hey, honey," he said, pulling her into a hug once he took the tray from her hands. "How are you, pet?"

"I'm fine, Daddy. Cupcake?"

"Were these specially made by you and Mary?"

"Of course. We'd never serve crap out of the store."

"You two need to open up your own bakery. Your both talented, hard workers, and these are worth paying for." Her father snagged a cupcake from the tray, biting into it. "Mm, delicious."

She blushed like she always did whenever she was paid a compliment. Her parents were always paying her compliments. Even when she was growing up they always found something to say about her.

"Stop your blushing. You deserve it." He kissed her cheek. "Don't you boys think so?"

Around the table were murmurs of agreement.

Picking up the tray she made her way around the table, handing everyone a cupcake. There was only one left by the time she got to Duke.

"Cupcake?" she asked, looking at the lonesome cake.

"Do you want it?"

She turned her gaze to his. Duke was the complete opposite of her in everything. Where she had blonde hair, his was black. Her eyes were blue, his were a dark brown. She licked her suddenly dry lips, wishing she was anywhere but beside him waiting for him to take a cupcake. There were times when she noticed his attention on her. She didn't know what to do about it. Should she do anything about it or just leave it? He had her confused.

"No. I've had enough cupcakes already."

She didn't need anything more to make her ass wider. Holly didn't mind her curves, and her mother had taught her at a young age not to be embarrassed by her body. Considering her parents were part of one of the strongest MCs around, they'd raised her to have morals and to care about others. Some MCs were not so considerate of others.

Duke took the cupcake from the tray. "It's good to see you around here."

Holly was around the clubhouse regularly, but she had been trying to take a back step for some time. She didn't want to become a biker's woman or old lady. Unlike her mother, who loved being an old lady, Holly hated the term. She refused to become part of the men's life. Instead, she'd started dating the deputy, who was a good ten years older than she was, but he treated her nice. He gave her flowers, which was a nice touch. The other great thing about Deputy Phil was he didn't talk constantly about the club. She'd been surprised on their first date. Holly had only told Mary about her date with

Phil. If her father caught wind of her dating anyone, he always gave them the third degree. The last thing she wanted was Phil anywhere near was her father and the club.

"I better take these to the kitchen." She hated him focusing on her. Duke could have any woman he wanted, and did have any woman he wanted. Holly heard the club whores talking. She wasn't an idiot about what went down in the clubhouse even if her father did try to keep it from her. Raoul had made sure she knew every little detail of what went on in the clubhouse.

Holly wasn't interested in becoming another whore for the club, nor did she want to become an old lady.

She passed Mary on the way toward the kitchen. "Are you okay?"

"I'm fine." She offered her friend a smile, disappearing inside. Holly put the serving tray on the table beside the mound of cupcakes she and Mary had prepared. There were enough to feed a small army. In the club it wouldn't take five minutes before they were gone.

Pressing her palm against her head, Holly let out a small breath.

"It's okay. It's completely okay. Everything is fine."

"Who are you trying to convince?"

She jumped, turning around to find Duke in the kitchen. How had he gotten in without her hearing him? The door was closed behind him.

"What?"

"That everything is okay. Who are you trying to convince?" He stood with one hand in his pocket, the other with his palm up, pointing toward her.

"No one." She stared down at the ground.

Neither of them spoke for several seconds. Holly returned her gaze to his, staring at him.

Her heart raced, and she couldn't control what was happening to her. Nipples budding, warmth spilled from her pussy as she became instantly attracted and aroused by the man before her. The wrong kind of man. This was the man who'd taken over from her father. She didn't want to have anything to do with him, yet her body was demanding his attention. Holly didn't know what to do to stop it.

Chapter Two

Holly may be fighting her attraction toward him, but Duke didn't have a problem letting her know what he wanted. This was the first time in months he'd gotten her alone. Stepping closer into the room, he'd made sure the door to the kitchen was locked. No one was going to disturb them, especially with Pike standing at the door. In this stage of the game with Holly, he needed her to be relaxed before he even considered taking the next step.

She didn't back away from him. The table was directly behind her, but that wouldn't stop her from moving away. He stepped close enough to her so that she could reach up and push him away if she chose.

"Hello, Holly."

"What do you want, Duke?"

He liked his name on her lips. There was something hot about hearing his name come from those full, tempting lips. He loved her lips. Every time he looked at them he couldn't help but see his cock sliding between them. She'd look good with his dick in her mouth, relishing his taste. Reaching out, he ran the tip of his thumb along her bottom lip. Holly gasped yet didn't pull away.

This woman before him was too innocent for her own good. She should run far away from him. But he'd find her. Duke would always find her. From the moment he took over the Trojans he'd seen Holly in a whole new light. She was a beautiful woman. Many men didn't like the full figured body, but he loved it. He'd taken his fair share of slender women who were skin and bones. Julie, his ex-wife, was one of those women. He'd also had to deal with the women telling him to stop because he was hurting them. Duke liked to grip his woman. There was nothing better than holding onto his woman and giving her the pounding she needed. Holly looked like she could take his strength. Not only could she take his strength, she'd bruise with his mark.

"You've got no idea what I want to do to these lips, do you?" He stared at her lips pressing his thumb between them. She did nothing but look at him. When he was about to withdraw he paused as the tip of her tongue glided over his thumb, tasting him.

There was a spark in her dilated eyes. Her nipples pressed against the thin shirt she wore, begging for him to touch, to stroke.

She took several deep breaths making her tits rise and fall. Sliding his fingers away from her mouth, he caressed around to her neck, touching her pulse, which was beating rapidly. Holly was affected by his presence. Her complete disregard was a lie. Duke saw it as he stared back at her.

Cupping her face with both hands, he tilted her head back to stare into her eyes. He waited for her to deny him, yet again she didn't. Duke slid his right hand away from her chin down to her collarbone. Staring into her eyes, he breezed down until he circled the hard bud of her nipple.

"Duke?"

"Tell me to stop." He raised a brow waiting for her to tell him to stop.

"What are you doing?" she asked.

"You think you can run and hide from me." He cupped her breast in his palm, sliding his finger over her hard nipple. Her deep breaths turned into short pants as he continued to touch her. Duke leaned in close brushing his lips against her ear. "Dating the deputy to pretend you don't belong to the club."

She jerked her head back. "How do you know who I was dating?"

He smiled. "Baby, I didn't earn my status by being slow. I know everything that goes down, including the fact the deputy has been buying you flowers. He treated you nice?"

Holly nodded her head.

If Phil hadn't he'd have visited the bastard. The Sheriff and deputy were in his pocket, taking his hard earned cash to stay out of their fucking business.

One of those businesses was knowing exactly where Holly was at all times. His need had turned into an obsession.

"Has he kissed you?" He'd break the bastard's fucking legs if he so much as touched her. Duke knew there was something going on with Phil. He didn't know what it was, but he'd find out. Dating Holly, Russ's daughter, came with a shitload of suspicion, especially if they were the law.

"No."

Closing that small distance between them, he pressed up against her. He wasn't wearing a jacket, and neither of them was wearing clothes that would obstruct how they felt against each other. Reaching around her, he held her steady as he thrust his cock against her stomach. He was so hard and ready to fuck her. Duke knew he was going to be inside Holly and soon. He'd waited long enough to claim her and to show Russ the respect. Duke wasn't going to wait any longer.

It wouldn't be long before someone else saw what a gem she was.

"Anyone else but Raoul?"

She gasped, trying to jerk back. He wouldn't let her move.

"Answer me."

"No."

Slamming his lips down on hers, Duke took the first kiss from her lips. He didn't let up from his touch, sliding his tongue into her mouth. Holly stayed still within his arms. She didn't do anything for so long. He sank his fingers into her hair, gripping on the length, tilting her head to get closer to her.

Her fingers started at his waist, sliding up his chest. Duke expected her to push him away. Instead, she gripped him a little harder, her fingers tightening in his shirt as gripped her hair tightly.

Duke broke from the kiss, seeing her lips were red and swollen already. Pushing the tray she placed on the table away from him, he picked her up and placed her on the edge. She let out a little squeal, laughing as he put her on the table top.

"You're going to pull a disc or something," she said.

In answer, Duke took possession of her lips, deepening the kiss. He stepped between her spread thighs, pressing his palm against her crotch. She gasped, pulling back from him. Had he gone too far? Duke didn't care. He'd taken his time, given her a chance to be ready. If Pike knew what was going on inside his head, Holly had to be aware.

There was a knock on the door interrupting their moment. Duke had been about to talk to Holly, but instead he looked over his shoulder toward the sound. "What?" His cock was rock hard, pressing against his zipper.

"Sorry to bother you, Duke. Matthew is looking for you," Pike said.

That was all it took for Holly to start pushing him away, getting firmer with each shove. "Get off me," she said, whispering out the words through gritted teeth. Duke growled. He was annoyed at being interrupted.

Stepping back, he watched her slide off the table glaring at him. She looked totally adorable when she was angry. "Go and find Matthew. This was a complete mistake."

Banding an arm around her waist, he slid down to grip her ass hard. "Baby, the only mistake that happened right now is the fact I had to fucking stop."

She pressed her palms against his chest to push him away. Duke was bigger and stronger than she was. "Keep trying, baby. You're not going to be the one in control. I am."

"Get your hands off me, Duke."

He glared at her. "Don't fucking think you can pretend you didn't want me, Holly. Your nipples are rock hard, and I bet your pussy is soaking wet, begging for my cock."

"You're crude."

"No, I'm fucking honest. Tell me you're not turned on." When she went to open her mouth, he put his own on hers, silencing her. "You better be prepared to prove a dry cunt, Holly," he said, breaking from the kiss.

She stayed silent as he waited for her to dispute his claim.

He took hold of her hand, pressing her palm against his cock. "This, Holly, it isn't over. Don't leave the clubhouse. We're going to have a talk." Duke took a step away from her, heading toward the door.

"Nothing is going on between us. One kiss means nothing."

Spinning back around, he stalked toward her. In three easy strides he stood in front of her. He didn't give her a chance to escape. Turning her in his arms so her back was to his front, he slid his hands inside the jeans she wore. He moved past the elastic of her jeans, sinking his fingers through her creamy slit. Duke groaned as she was bare to the touch. He'd not been expecting his woman to be completely bare, maybe a small patch of curls but not bare. "I'm going to be licking this beautiful little cunt, Holly." He rubbed his finger around her slick clit before diving down to sink his fingers inside her sweet little pussy. "Fuck, baby, you're wetter than even I imagined." Duke groaned as he slid two fingers inside her with ease. She cried out, thrusting onto his fingers. "You can try and pretend all you want, Holly. I know the truth, and this is not the end."

He heard her swallow. "You need to go and deal with your son."

Pumping two digits into her core, he made her moan before he withdrew. With her gaze on him he brought his wet fingers to his mouth, and with her focused on him, he licked her cream right off. "You taste so fucking sweet."

"Your son?" She didn't sound sure about him leaving her alone.

"This isn't over, Holly. We're going to finish this *conversation*."

He released her then left the kitchen completely. Duke smiled as he headed toward Matthew. The taste of Holly was still on his tongue. It certainly wasn't over. In fact, it had only just begun.

****

Holly pressed a palm to her heart. What the hell had just happened? She couldn't believe Duke had just finger fucked her, and yet there was no other explanation for what the hell just happened.

Why didn't you push him away?
Why didn't you tell him to stop?

There was no reason that came to mind. The moment he got close to her all of her other functions shut down. It was like she wasn't herself. Mary entered the kitchen carrying her own tray of cupcakes.

"Hey you. Are you all right?"

Was she all right? She didn't know.

"I'm fine."

"Duke left here with a smile. Want to let me know what's going on?"

"No." She tucked the strands behind her ear. Her hands were shaking. He'd aroused her body and left. What the hell was she to do? There wasn't a chance of her taking home any of the men within the club. She still struggled to look at her father after she was with Raoul.

"Something went on, and you've got to tell me. I live through you."

Mary was still a virgin. They had both agreed to lose their virginity together. Holly failed in keeping to her word when Raoul put on the charm. She really thought he was real, and in fact, he was a bigger fake than anyone she'd ever met.

"Nothing, not much." Heat filled her cheeks, and no matter how much Mary begged, there was no way Holly could bring herself to say what actually happened.

"Okay, then just tell me that *something* happened."

"God, what are you, twelve? Yes, *something* happened, but I'm not telling you what."

"From the look of frustration on your face I'd say it was something dirty."

Holly forced herself to work putting the next layer of cupcakes onto the tray. She wouldn't look at her friend.

When the tray was filled she looked up as Mary put a hand on her shoulder. "Be careful, Holly. I love you like a sister. I'd hate to see you hurt."

Mary showed too much emotion. Anyone who took the time to get to know her would know she was a darling woman who'd not had a great life. Her parents couldn't give a shit about her. She worked her ass off as a waitress when she wasn't at their apartment trying out new recipes. Mary and Holly had a strong friendship that had built over the years, and they were loyal to each other. They also had a great love of food and baking.

"I won't let anything happen."

"Are you sure? You look more frazzled than you did when you were with Raoul."

Holly scrunched up her nose. "God, I hate that man."

"He's a loser, Hols. Don't worry, I'll make sure he suffers."

She burst out laughing at Mary's threat. "You couldn't hurt a fly."

"I could bloody try. He hurt my girl."

Wrapping her arms around Mary's waist, she chuckled. "Love you, Mary."

"Love you, too. Now, let's get this show on the road before they start eating each other."

"You watch way too many movies."

Mary shrugged. Together they made their way out. Instead of passing out the cupcakes, Holly put her tray in the center of the table, pulling away as hands started to take the cupcakes. Her mother, Sheila, came to stand next to her.

"You did well today, honey. Your father is proud."

Nodding, Holly leaned her head on her mother's shoulder. Her gaze moved across the clubhouse garden to see Duke and Julie arguing. She looked for Matthew to see him shooting hoops in the small court her father had built when her mother had been expecting a boy. An attack on the Trojans had made her mother lose her baby brother and also stop Sheila from having any more kids. It had affected her parents, and she was sure her father had found comfort in the whores available at the club, but that was some years ago.

Sheila never talked about it with her. Club business, including relationships, stayed within the club. Her mother wouldn't tell her young daughter about what happened. Since the miscarriage, her parents hadn't really been the same. She knew Russ loved her mother, but there was sadness in his eyes whenever he let his guard down. The only thing that kept them together was their love for each other.

"Honey, I want to talk to you about something."

"Can it wait? I just want to go and see someone." She pulled away from Sheila to make her way toward Matthew. "Is that okay?"

"Yeah, baby. Go on."

She smiled at her mother then made her way across the clubhouse garden toward the court. Leaning against the fence, she stared at Matthew as he kept shooting the ball and missing.

In the distance she heard Duke arguing with Julie.

"You're a fucking slut. Your son is here, and you're trying to pick men up."

"I'm not your bitch anymore."

"Thank fuck for that."

"Hey," Holly said, moving toward the young boy. He was fourteen years old, and he looked like a younger version of his dad. There was no sign of Julie in the boy, which was a blessing. Even Sheila couldn't stand Julie.

"Hey," Matthew said, rolling the ball between his hands.

"You okay?"

"I don't need any pity!" He glared up at her, showing her the anger simmering beneath the surface.

Holding her hands up in surrender, she backed up a step. "Whoa, I'm not showing you any pity, but I

25

figured as you've failed to shoot the ball into the hoop, you need to talk."

"What the fuck could you have to say?"

Raising a brow, Holly glanced around her. No one was paying them any attention. Stepping closer, she snatched the ball out of Matthew's hand.

"Oh, I don't think the little Duke saw that one coming." She started to bounce the ball in front of her. Matthew made a charge at her. Grabbing the ball, she spun on her foot, dodging his attack and moving closer to the hoop.

"Lucky," Matthew said. "Bet you can't get it through the hoop."

"Okay." She faced the hoop, bounced the ball twice, and threw the ball. Holly jumped up and down, whooping as the ball went clean through the hoop.

"First time luck."

"Aren't you a little young to be so cynical?"

Matthew threw the ball at her. She caught it with ease.

"Shoot again."

Cocking her head to the side, she rolled her eyes, shooting the ball straight through the hoop a second time. Matthew stood by the hoop looking pretty shocked. She walked up to him, bending down to grab the ball. Leaning in close, she thrust the ball against his chest, which Matthew grabbed.

"You're not the only kid who grew up with a parent being a president." She made sure she had Matthew's gaze on her. His gaze focused on her chest. *Great, like father like son.* Bending down so that she was no longer leaning over for him to get an eyeful of her tits, Holly caught his attention onto her face this time. "Stop being a wimp. Your parents are going to argue, but it's not your fault."

"You spent a lot of time shooting hoops?"

"Honey, I lived on this court. I made Mary so mad, even though she can shoot hoops nearly as good as I can. Don't let them affect you, Matthew. You're just a boy. Stop being cynical, and if you curse at me again, I'll make sure you know what it means to be punished."

"You'd hit me?"

"No, honey, there's more than hitting to a punishment. Cleaning toilets, shoveling dog shit, or the worst, doing the dishes, and there's a lot of dishes."

The horror on his face made her chuckle.

"I won't curse at you."

"Good." She tapped the ball, standing up, and making her way toward Mary.

Duke stopped her before she could leave. Holly had been so focused on the boy she'd not even heard him stop arguing with his ex.

"What?" she asked, waiting for him to say some shit about what went down in the kitchen.

"Thanks."

"What for?"

"Talking with Matthew."

"You've got to stop fighting with his mother in front of him. There's a lot of anger inside him." She stared down at where he held her arm. Holly hated the way she was easily affected by his touch. She shouldn't like his touch so much.

The remembered feel of his fingers inside her had her breath catching as she looked at him. From the look in his eyes, she knew he was thinking about what had gone down in the kitchen.

"He's a good kid."

"But he's still a kid, Duke. It won't be long until he's blaming himself for your divorce."

"Not keeping her thighs closed to a dick is what got the divorce."

He pulled her close to him, and Holly placed a hand on his chest. "Let me go."

She looked toward the tables to see if they'd caught anyone's attention. No one paid them any. Mary was standing by a swing, and she saw Pike was trying to talk to her.

"You don't want anyone to know about us?"

"There's no us."

Returning her gaze to his dark one, Holly gasped as he rested his palm against her neck. The tips of his fingers brushed across her pulse, which pounded at his touch. Everything and everyone fell away as she stared at Duke, waiting for him to make the next move. He did nothing as he looked at her apart from stroking her neck.

Licking her lips, Holly gasped as he came closer. His breath fanned across her face.

"There is, Holly. You want to keep this a secret then fine, but you're not getting away from me."

"Why now?" She'd been dating Phil for a couple of weeks. In all the time she'd been at the club, Duke had never shown any interest in her. Sure, she knew he looked at her, a lot, but he'd shown no other sign.

"You're ready now."

"You're older than I am."

"Do you care?"

Biting into her bottom lip, Holly was tempted to lie.

"Answer me, Holly."

"No, I don't care." She couldn't bring herself to lie to him.

"Good. I'll keep us a secret for now, but you better not think to run from me or to hide."

She pulled her arm away. Duke held her arm long enough for her to know that he was the one in control of things today.

Holly didn't answer him. What was the point? Duke was used to people bowing down to him, giving him what he wanted. The club pussy talked a great deal about how he was in bed. She wasn't interested in becoming one in a long line of women.

A couple of weeks ago she'd told her mother she was staying out of the club life. Sheila had begged her to come for the celebrations today. She'd not wanted to, but when her mother started to beg, Holly couldn't deny her.

Phil wasn't part of the club. She'd seen what the club had done to her parents' marriage and several other couples. The men cheated, the old ladies got hurt, and the club whores started to think they were something special. Holly wouldn't live that life of not knowing if her man was fucking someone else. Her biggest mistake had been screwing around with Raoul. She wouldn't make another one, including Duke. He'd be a big mistake. Once she fell for him, there really was no turning back.

Chapter Three

"Diaz wants this deal. The Mexicans are moving closer, and if we don't act now, we'll be fucked," Raoul said.

Duke sat in church listening to Raoul talk about the latest drug deal. He hated the drug runs, but they brought in a shitload of money and kept the Mexicans off his back and out of his town, Vale Valley.

Looking toward Russ, he knew the other man had done everything to keep the club safe. Being in with the Mexicans gave them some level of protection. They could handle their own against most attacks, but people didn't like to take on their associates.

"This is your deal now, Duke."

Running a hand down his face, he tapped his fingers on the table top. This was the part of being the president he hated. He had to have the final say that could put all of them at risk. The last thing he wanted was to have a brother's death on his conscience.

"Set up the meet. I want it out of town, neutral territory. Diaz has to be there."

Raoul agreed. "I'll set it up."

"I don't want anyone in our town risking our families." Duke looked at each man. The ones who didn't have families still knew it was important to keep them safe. When the Trojans retaliated they never took their revenge out on families. Gangs, street clubs, bad clubs, were the norm now in their world. The safety of families was not always a guarantee. "Anyone got a fucking issue with us continuing our drug runs?"

No one said a word. They all got a nice profit from running drugs and guns. Duke didn't like running the guns. It was far more dangerous than the drugs, or at least to him it was.

This meeting had been long overdue. Three days had passed since the Fourth of July celebrations, and it had been that long since he'd last seen Holly. The club had demanded his attention, but he'd put Daisy, one of the club members, onto her protection. Daisy was to stay out of sight so Holly didn't see him. Daisy was a guy but had gotten so damn drunk one night that he'd gotten a tattoo on his back of a big fuckoff daisy. Since that day he'd been known as Daisy. Anyone who tried to take on the mean-assed fucker learned their mistake. Daisy was at church, as were all of his men, so protection detail had been cancelled for the hour of the meeting.

"Does anyone else have anything to bring to the table?"

Russ leaned forward. "I want to know what you're doing sniffing around Holly."

Duke stared at Holly's father, the previous president of the Trojans. He had a shitload of respect for the man. Russ had been a great president and when he stepped down it was hard for Duke to take the lead, but he did it to lead the Trojans in the direction that Russ had.

"None of your business."

"It is my business when my girl calls me up and asks me why she's being tailed by an asshole sporting the insignia of our club." Their insignia was of a horse with two Glocks pointing toward each other. On the outside of the insignia, "Trojans" was across the top with "MC" along the bottom.

He looked toward Daisy, smirking. "You told me she didn't have a clue you were tailing her."

"My daughter is not a fucking idiot. She's lived her whole life having men on her tail for protection. Never underestimate Holly. She'll kick your ass."

"Holly's protection is my concern."

31

"She's my daughter. My only child, Duke. I demand respect or you pay the price. President or not, I take care of my family." Russ looked toward Raoul. "I almost lost her because of that asshole. I'm not going to risk losing her because you got a need to prove a point."

Pressing his palms on the table, Duke leaned in close to look at Russ. His palms being flat on the table was a sign he wasn't reaching for his gun to show Russ who was boss. Facing Russ head on also showed him he wasn't backing the fuck down.

"I'm not playing around with Holly."

"Then what the fuck are you going to do?"

All of the men were looking at him, waiting. They cared about Holly, but it was up to him what he made of Holly. If he took her as a club whore, she became fair game. They would all give her the respect she earned and because she was Russ's daughter, but it would be up to her what she did. If he took her as his old lady, they'd all know not to touch her.

"She doesn't want anyone to know. Nothing has happened, and the only reason I'm telling you, Russ, is out of mutual respect. Holly will be mine."

"What about Julie? Fucking whore will hurt my girl if given the chance."

"Leave her to me. No one will hurt Holly, and I can promise you I won't be driving her away from the club."

"Good luck with that. Holly's doing everything she can to steer clear. Her mother's trying to talk to her, but so far, she's not listening."

Duke nodded. "I don't want any of you to make a fucking sound of what's discussed here. You do, and you're out. If church can't stay fucking sacred, then you can't be trusted to keep our deals quiet."

Each man murmured their agreement.

"Dismissed." He slammed the gavel down calling a close to the meeting. Like all the times before, Duke stayed in his chair while everyone made their way out of the room. Russ stayed back just like Duke knew he would.

"What, Russ?"

"Holly's been part of the club all of her life. I never hid anything from her. She knows most of what goes down."

"Funny, does she know what taking an old lady is like?"

"No. Like I said, she knows most of what goes on but not all. I expect you to keep me out of it whatever you decide." Russ made his way toward the door. "Don't turn her into a club whore. That's all I ask. Father to father and shit like that. I know you have a son, but think about it."

Duke stared at the older man.

"The club is yours, and I'm not asking you as a club member. I'm asking you as a father. Don't turn my little girl into a whore."

"You and I both know Holly's not got what it takes to be a whore." That was all he was going to say on the matter. He watched Russ leave the room. Sitting back, Duke ran a finger across his bottom lip. He'd kept his distance from Holly, allowing her the chance to get over whatever shit was going on in her head from Raoul.

Grabbing his keys, he made his way out of the office toward the main door. One of the latest club whores was sliding up and down the strip pole the boys had insisted getting. Pike sat drinking a beer, watching the fake blonde as she gave him her best come on face.

Duke walked out of the clubhouse toward his bike, which was chained to the metal pole near their mechanics front. Duke made sure to employ several townies who knew how to work cars and bikes. No one but himself fixed his own bike.

"I'm sorry, man," Daisy said, coming to stand beside him.

"No problem. I should have known Holly would know you were following her."

"She didn't give me any shit."

"Don't worry about it. Is today her day off?"

"Yeah."

"What about Mary?" The two women lived together in a modest apartment near the center of town. It was far enough away from the clubhouse that if someone ever needed her, they'd have to come to her. Last time he checked neither woman could drive. Russ lived a couple miles from the club in a little condo set back from the beaten track. Many of the boys had houses around Vale Valley that were only a short distance from the clubhouse. Duke had bought an old ranch house, and when he wasn't at the club or dealing with his son and ex, he was restoring it back to its former glory. He loved getting his hands dirty and getting stuck into a project. For as long as he could remember he had always loved creating things with his hands. He'd been the one to make the table with the club's insignia on it. No one in the club knew who created the table but him and Russ.

"She's working a double shift at the diner. Mac has got her working hard. He's trying to get into her pants so she'll help him run the diner."

Mac Reynolds owned the local diner. He was in his thirties and had taken over from his parents. It was no secret that Mary was one hell of a cook. All of her potlucks were successes. The club loved having her around just for her food. Duke wondered what Pike thought of Mac's interest.

"Does she show any sign of wanting anything to do with him?"

"Not last time I checked. She kept her distance. Doesn't even date."

Duke frowned. "How the fuck did you find that one out?"

"I was in the diner sitting in a booth close to Holly and Mary. They were talking, arguing about Mary's lack of a social life."

Holly cared about her friend. He'd have to have a word with Pike. If the fucker didn't act soon he'd have a pissed off VP, and that wasn't something he looked forward to. Pike pissed off was not a sight anyone wanted to live to see. It was deadly, dangerous, and fucked up. People died when Pike got upset.

"Pike's going to be pissed if anything happens to Mary."

Daisy held his hands up. "I'm just the messenger, and you've got to love the club."

"Thanks." He shook Daisy's hand. "When are you going to get your tat removed?"

"Remove my ink? I fucking love Daisy. Gives me an edge."

Laughing, Duke climbed on his bike, firing it up. Firing up the engine, he loved the feel of the machine vibrating beneath him.

"Have fun."

He was going to have a lot of fun.

****

"Shit, ouch, fuck, sugar hot. Ouch." Holly dropped the wooden spoon down onto the counter with a clatter. Rushing over to the tap, she plunged her fingers into the warm water. She'd been working with some toffee, but so far everything she tried to do was a mess.

There wasn't a chance of her making any pretty hearts or even some leaves. "Stupid toffee."

She pulled her hand out of the water and saw the tips of her fingers were red. Moving back to the designs on the tray, she scribbled out the recipe she'd been working on with Mary. The sound of the doorbell ringing had her frowning. Holly checked the clock to see it wasn't anywhere close to ten o'clock when Mary got off work. It was her one day off from the nursery, and she was spending the time trying out new recipes. She couldn't think of a better way to spend her day. The morning had been a nightmare of cleaning up last night's mess. Mary wanted to work pineapple into a cake recipe that had a strong taste. Every recipe they'd tried had been a failure.

The doorbell rang once again.

"I'm coming."

Glancing down at her flour covered shirt, which also had grease stains from the butter she used, Holly shrugged. She wasn't going to rush off and change. It was probably the delivery man. She'd tied her hair up on top of her head to keep it out of her way as she worked her magic.

Opening the door without glancing through the peephole she stopped as she saw Duke standing on her doorstep.

"What are you doing here?" It had been three days since their little kiss in the kitchen.

Nothing about that kiss was little.

"It's about time I stopped by."

"Is this about Daisy?" She stopped him from entering by stepping in the gap and keeping the door close to her side. The only way he was getting into her apartment was if he forced his way inside. She lived on the second floor, but the building wasn't all that secure.

Anyone could come and go as they pleased. He didn't need her permission to buzz his way inside.

"No."

"Who put him on my ass?"

"I did."

There was no remorse in his eyes or in his stance.

"Why?"

"My woman stays protected at all times."

"I'm not your woman. Why do you keep saying that?"

He stepped closer. She gripped the door a little tighter. Holly was no match for his strength if he decided to take what he wanted and move her aside.

"You're my woman, Holly. My woman has protection."

"Julie doesn't." She purposefully brought up his ex. Julie was a horrid person. Holly couldn't stand her.

"She's a whore. She's not my concern."

"She's the mother of your child."

Duke burst out laughing.

"Baby, she hasn't ever been a mother to Matthew."

He slid his hand across her waist. His touch made her pause as she looked at him. What could she say to him? Julie *wasn't* a mother to Matthew. Holly knew she'd been caught fucking another man in their bed.

"Now, you can either let me inside where we can have some privacy or we can do all of this for anyone to see. We can keep it out in the open for everyone to know it's me here."

Pulling out of his touch, she stepped away from the front door. She turned on her heel, heading back to the kitchen. Holly was sure she heard a groan from behind her. When she glanced back at Duke, she saw his gaze on her ass. She wore a pair of shorts that went to her knees, but they were the kind that molded to the shape of her ass.

"Perv," she said. His gaze gave her a thrill that she didn't want to have.

Stop thinking about him. He's not important.

She released a little groan of her own when she saw the toffee had stuck. It was going to be a bitch to scrub off. Screwing up the disasters that were supposed to be toffee she threw them in the trash with the greaseproof paper. Dumping the saucepan in the sink, she turned on the hot water to put it in to soak. All the time she was working, she was aware of him in her small kitchen. Her apartment was small and modest. She and Mary couldn't afford anything bigger. Russ had offered to get her a bigger place, already paid for, but there would have been no chance of getting Mary to live with her. Mary wouldn't accept any charity and preferred to earn her keep rather than have it handed to her on a plate.

Drying her hands, Holly was about to turn around when Duke placed his hands on either side of the kitchen counter trapping her in. He was larger than she was. If she was to lean back her head would be at his chest.

"You like me being a perv. I seem to recall a certain creamy pussy."

She closed her eyes, trying to fight the budding arousal he was inspiring. Holly didn't want to give into the need he was creating.

"Why are you here?"

"It has been three days."

"So?"

"I've given you long enough to deal with the thought of us. I couldn't hold back any longer." His lips nuzzled her neck.

Holly couldn't hold back her gasp as he licked the pulse beating against her neck. Opening her eyes, she stared out of the kitchen window. She didn't see anything in front of her. Gripping the counter tightly she released a moan as one of his hands landed on her rounded stomach.

"Mary's coming home soon."

"No, she's not. You're alone for most of the day. Mary's doing double shifts at the diner. You know I could make that stop."

"She likes working at the diner."

"Does she like Mac drooling all over her?" he asked.

"He's a nice guy." Mac didn't force the issue with Mary. The guy had only made his desire for her friend known.

"Mary belongs to Pike."

"Mary belongs to no one, just like I don't."

"That's where you're wrong, baby. You belong to me." The hand that had been resting on her stomach moved down to cup her pussy through her shorts. "This pussy is all mine."

He rubbed his fingers through her shorts, pressing against her clit.

"I believe I left you unsatisfied the last time we were together."

She whimpered as he stopped touching her. The hand that had touched her intimately through her shorts, now touched her face. He turned her so she had no choice but to look at him. "I'm going to take care of that need for you now, baby."

Holly should push him away.

"Give me those lips."

Duke had always intrigued her for as long as she could remember. Even when he was married to Julie, there had been that draw to him. Holly didn't understand it. He touched her, and she went up in flames at his touch.

He leaned forward, and Holly couldn't resist. The moment his lips were on hers, she was burning with need. After he'd worked her up toward an orgasm yet given her nothing, she'd come home and tried to find release at her own hand. She'd failed. No matter how much she touched herself, she couldn't bring herself off.

Three days she'd been unsatisfied, but Duke kisses her once and that was it. She was dying for more.

His tongue traced along her bottom lip. Opening her mouth she touched his tongue with her own. She tasted the coffee on his lips but not the staleness of cigarettes. Did Duke smoke? She didn't know nor did she care. Reaching up, she sank her fingers into his hair, drawing him deeper. He slid his tongue deep into her mouth, meeting each stroke. She imagined his cock would be the same, fucking her hard.

Groaning, she turned in his arms and ran her hands beneath the leather of his cut. She shoved the jacket off his body as Duke grabbed her ass. There was no way she could contain the need any longer. Three days of frustration, three days of being denied release, and Holly no longer held onto any sense. She needed him to put out the fire that he'd built.

He turned her back to the table. With one swoop of his hand, he sent flour, sugar, cookery books, spoons, and a couple of metal bowls spilling to the floor. She didn't care. Later, she'd clean up the mess later. The only thing she could focus on right now was Duke. He lifted her up and placed her down on the table. Tearing open his belt, Holly gasped as he pressed on her chest, forcing her to lie back. His hands slid down her chest, circling her nipples as he glided down to her shorts.

She went to her elbows and watched as he easily opened the button of her shorts.

"I'm the one in charge. I'm the one in control. Not you, baby. Me." He stepped between her splayed legs, gripping either side of her shorts. She stared into his eyes, as he worked the material down her legs. The shorts were white, and she'd chosen underwear that wouldn't show through. She wore a white lace thong and a bra to match.

"Fuck, baby." His palm covered her pussy. He rubbed her through the panties. Fisting her hands, she cried out, whimpering as he parted the lips of her sex. The panties slid between creating a slightly rough edge to touch her clit.

Duke ran his hands up and down her inner thighs.

"Your naked pussy makes me so fucking hard, baby."

She hated having to deal with pubic hair and kept herself cleanly shaven. Holly also liked the feel of being bare, and the touch of her panties and clothes as she worked never failed to turn her on.

He worked her shirt up going over her breasts. Duke didn't remove her bra, but he pulled the cups down so that her breasts fell freely out.

Keeping her gaze locked on him, she bit her lip as he tugged his shirt over his head. His body was covered in ink. She'd seen him without a shirt before. On his back he wore the insignia of the club. The members who got "Trojans MC" inked onto their backs had no intention of leaving. Duke, he wasn't going anywhere. He was part of the club to stay. It was his life, like the air he breathed. The club was what he needed to live. Her heart pounded inside her chest. She remembered one summer when she was seventeen. Her mother had sent her to the clubhouse to study as they had decorators in to fit the new kitchen. Mary was working and couldn't spend the day with her. Holly had spent the day out in the sun with her books open on the ground around her. Leaning up against a tree the guys had left her alone. It had been hot, and the guys had decided to have a game of basketball. She'd sat watching as all men removed their shirts, playing to the game.

Duke had glanced her way. She'd been unable to look away, drawing her knees up to her chest as he stared right back. He'd given her a smile before carrying on. It couldn't have been for longer than a couple of minutes, yet she'd felt that gaze for a long time. Her pussy had grown slick. He was older than she was, and it still hadn't stopped the attraction.

His hands moved to his belt, and within seconds he was working his jeans down his thighs.

Arousal, hard and thick gripped her, tightening things deep into her stomach.

"Are you on the pill?"

This was going to happen.

Chapter Four

Duke stroked his cock, staring at her naked body. He couldn't wait long enough to grab a condom nor could he wait to take this into the bedroom. Three days he'd been without her. It had been well over a year since he'd taken any club pussy. The moment he realized he was going to have Holly as his old lady, he'd stopped banging every other pussy. He'd known she wouldn't like him to have been screwing around. The only person she'd been with was Raoul. After the incident, without Russ's orders, he'd kept an eye on her. The men and boys who'd been sniffing around her had gotten a warning from him. He didn't share in any way.

"Yes, I'm on the pill."

In one tug he tore the white panties from her body. He pushed them into his jeans pocket. They were his trophy for today. The sight of her naked pussy was nearly his undoing. Thirty-nine years old and he was ready to come at the sight of her cunt. The lips of her sex were open, revealing her swollen clit. Cream covered her slit and coated her lips. Running his finger through her pussy, he circled the nub, before sliding down to thrust inside her.

She cried out.

"Fuck, baby. I've got to have a taste."

He placed her feet on the edge of the table, opening her thighs a little wider. Going to his knees, he opened her pussy with his fingers. Within seconds he sucked her clit into his mouth.

She screamed, arching up off the table. Pressing his palm against her stomach, he forced her to stay down. He was stronger than she was. With his hand on her stomach, he kept her still as he ravished her pussy. Flicking his tongue over her clit, he circled the hard bud before sliding down to plunge into her tight, hot cunt. She was so fucking tasty and wet. He didn't suck women's pussy, especially the club whores'. Duke didn't want to risk licking another guy's semen. Holly was pure. It had been years since she'd been with Raoul, and she'd not been with anyone else. A great wave of possession overcame him. Holly was going to be all his. He'd not had a woman who'd not been fucked by multiple men before. Gripping her hips, he held her in place as he fucked her several times with his tongue.

"Fuck, Duke," she said, moaning.

He loved hearing her pleasured cries. Duke released his hold on one of her hips, to move down to press two fingers into her pussy. She tried to thrust down onto his fingers. He worked them inside her, harder. When they were coated in her cream, he eased them down to the puckered hole of her anus. She tensed up beneath him.

"Has my baby not been fucked in the ass?"

She groaned.

"Well?"

"No."

"Then you're going to be in for a surprise because I'm going to fuck this ass."

"Isn't it wrong?"

"No, baby. You're going to fucking love the feel of my cock in your ass." He stroked over her puckered hole, slowing his caresses so she started to crave his touch more than anything else. She started to relax. He continued tonguing her clit alternatively fucking into her pussy with his tongue. When she was completely relaxed, he pressed the tip of his finger to her hot ass. The tight muscles kept him out.

He wasn't going to denied what he wanted, and he wanted her to open up to him like a flower in summer.

"Duke."

"Let me in, Holly. Trust me."

She whimpered.

Pressing his finger to her anus, the tight ring of muscles still kept him out.

"Push out," he said.

She did as he ordered, and he eased his finger into her ass. Holly tensed up and tried to get away from him. Standing up, he kept one hand on her stomach while he worked his finger inside her ass.

"Feel me."

When she didn't try to get away from him, he moved the hand on her stomach down to tease her clit. He gave her the double pleasure of touching her clit as well as teasing her ass. In time he'd have her begging to take his cock. Until the time was right, he'd get her used to his touch. Every time she tried to forget about him, Duke was determined to give her a little reminder of who he was.

"Please."

"Do you need to come?"

"Yes."

"Then ask me."

"Please, Duke, I need to come. Let me come."

He smiled. Moving his fingers to her cunt, he pressed two inside her as he worked her clit with his thumb. Duke stared into her eyes and watched as she splintered apart under his touch. He'd kept her at the edge so that it didn't take long to have her going over.

She cried out, arching up, thrusting against his touch. He pulled his fingers out of her ass, grabbing the towel from the floor to wipe his fingers before he touched her further.

When she came down from her orgasm, he rubbed the tip of his cock through her slit. The rounded, bulbous tip was coated in his pre-cum. He was so turned on that he feared he'd come inside her with a few easy thrusts. Duke knew how to make those few thrusts worth it.

He stared down at where his cock separated her pussy lips. Duke wasn't a small man. He was large, and he knew the first thrust might hurt her. Bringing her to orgasm before fucking her had been the only idea for him. If he fucked her now, he was going to hurt her, and hurt her bad.

She was small compared to him, and her pussy was incredibly tight.

Wrapping his fingers around the base of his cock, he guided the tip to her entrance. He couldn't look anywhere else. Her cream was leaking out of her making his penetration easy. Gritting his teeth, he pushed the head of his cock inside her. With only the tip of his cock within her pussy, he felt how tight she was going to be. Slowly, inch by inch, he worked his way into her pussy.

Holly cried out. Glancing up, he saw her eyes were wide as she stared back at him.

"You're hurting me," she said, shaking.

Reaching between them with his gaze on her, he stroked her clit. She let out a gasp, and her eyes were dilated.

"You're big."

"I know, baby. You'll get used to my size." He'd spend the rest of his life fucking her in order for her to get used to the feel of him. Stroking her clit with one hand, he used the other to caress her body. He glided his fingers up her quivering stomach, to circle her nipples. She was such a sensitive woman. Duke had noticed her response when he touched her neck, stroked her body or brushed up against her.

She started to thrust up to meet his cock. He waited until she was the one working his dick into her tight cunt. Duke was a patient man, and within minutes he was rewarded by her begging him to move.

"Please, Duke."

"You want me to fuck you?"

"Yes, please, I need it."

Returning his hands to her hips, he slammed inside her to the hilt. Holly arched up, screaming as he went to the hilt inside her. He hit the top of her cervix, and she'd taken the whole of his cock. Duke tightened his hold on her hips, wanting to mark her skin so every time she saw them, she'd know who she belonged to.

He didn't want her to forget him. Duke intended to fill her pussy, claim her ass, and leave his mark on her body.

Sliding out of her pussy, he watched his cock, slick with her cream, reappear. The sight was so fucking hot it had his balls tightening up. Gritting his teeth, he slammed inside her, growling as her pussy tightened around him. Her cunt fluttered around his length, squeezing the life out of him.

"Your pussy is so fucking tight."

She moaned, wrapping her legs around his waist, and pulled him in.

"Harder," she said.

Duke didn't question her. Tightening his fingers on her hips so that they were white from the grip, he rammed into her. The table started to move from the force of his thrusts. Annoyed, he pulled out of her, grabbing a chair. In quick moves he pulled her onto his lap, gripped his cock, and was back inside her as she straddled his lap. Her hands went to his shoulders. "I'm going to fuck you in the clubhouse on the table in church."

"I'm not allowed there," she said, moving up and down his length.

He held her ass this time, squeezing the flesh. Duke used his strength to guide her over his length. She sank down on him in hard thrusts that had them both crying out in pleasure.

"You will be as my woman."

She pressed a hand to his mouth. "Stop talking."

He grinned, taking over control, and fucking her using her body for his pleasure.

"You're not the one in control here, Holly. I am."

Duke didn't hold anything back, showing her his strength, and making her take the whole of his cock. She gasped, bit her lip, and looked totally out of control as he fucked her. He watched her tits bounce and forced his hips up.

She reached between them to stroke her clit. Gritting his teeth, Duke held off his orgasm for her to find her own release. She came with a few strokes, and Duke followed her spilling his cum deep into her womb.

When it was over, she collapsed over him, pressing her head to his shoulder. He ran his hands up and down her back.

"I'm not going to be your old lady."

"You will." There wasn't a chance in hell he was letting her get away.

****

Holly climbed off his lap, and without looking back at him, she made her way toward her shower. The apartment was modest in the living space, but when it came to the bedrooms it was a little more luxurious as she and Mary had separate bathrooms. When they went hunting for an apartment they could have picked one with a larger kitchen and living space, but they both wanted their own bathrooms so they forfeited the larger living space for hygiene. There was only a shower, toilet, and sink within the room. Holly preferred it like this. She'd rather not share a bathroom with anyone. From a young age she liked her own bathroom. It probably came from stumbling into the bathroom when her parents were fucking in the shower.

Nothing screamed privacy more than seeing your father's dick in places you'd rather not.

Turning on the water, she stepped under the spray, wishing for some sanity over what just happened.

Holy fuck, I've just fucked Duke Bana, president of the Trojans MC.

She rubbed her hands over her face, hoping it was some awful dream.

It wasn't a dream. Her pussy ached from his hard cock. Duke wasn't a small man, and she knew all the gossip about his dick was true. Holly pressed her head against the wall, and the water sprayed down her back. Her ass hurt a little from his finger, but he'd gotten a response from her there as well. She hadn't been able to stop responding to his touch.

Duke set the flame of need burning inside her into an inferno. She couldn't put it out.

The bathroom door opened, and then the door to the shower stall did as well.

"You're not gone?" she asked. She half expected him to run off and brag about fucking her, like Raoul had.

"Why would I be gone?"

He reached around her, and she saw him pick up the soap. His hands were large, twice the size of hers. Duke was the first man to make her feel small in presence. It was nice. With him at her back she felt ... delicate.

Her mother had told her never to worry about her size. She always liked her food, and her mother was a good cook as was her grandma. Both Russ and Sheila had grown up in the club lifestyle as a member. Russ was the first man in his family who took the gavel. Sheila's parents, her grandparents, had simply been loyal members.

"Shouldn't you have some club work to do?" she asked. She couldn't bring herself to face him. His semen dripped down the inside of her thigh. Holly groaned. She'd not given a thought to ask him if he was clean.

"All club work was done before I came here."

She jumped as his hands went to her arms running up and down. They were covered in soap as he washed her.

"I'm not going to hurt you."

She closed her eyes. "You got what you wanted. Why don't you run back and tell the club about it? I bet they'll have a good laugh about how you got me to fuck you without much work."

His hands tightened on her arms. Holly cried out as his grip turned to pain. He spun her around fast and pressed her up against the wall. Duke grabbed her hands trapping them above her head, and he gripped her chin. There was nowhere for her to run.

"Let's get one thing straight, baby, I'm not and I'll never be like that fuck Raoul. I don't kiss and fucking tell. What happens between us, stays between us." His body was flush against her. Even flaccid she was aware of the length of his cock against her stomach. "I don't run to the club, nor do I use women. If I wanted the club to know who I was fucking, I'd tell them straight. I wouldn't disrespect you by making shit embarrassing for you. Let me make one thing clear. We're only a secret because you don't want anyone to know that your pussy creams at the sight of me."

"I hate you." She spat the words out. Holly hated him, but she hated herself even more. The power he held over her scared her. She didn't want to be easy, yet he was right. All it took was one look from him and she was ready.

"No, baby." The hand on her chin moved down her body to cup her pussy. He fucked two fingers into her pussy, and she closed her eyes groaning. "You don't hate me. You want me, and that's what you hate. You've been hurt by one of the club before, and you're scared. I'm not going to hurt you. My cum is inside your pussy, and that's where it's going to stay. You're not going to date any other man, and no cock is ever going to know how tight you are, do you understand me?"

"You're not the boss of me." Her voice didn't sound strong enough even to herself. The way he played her body was like she was his own personal toy. She wasn't a toy.

"Tell me again, baby, but this time make sure I can believe you." His thumb rubbed over her sensitive clit, making any argument she had before, non-existent. "You know you're mine. You've been mine for a long fucking time. We both know who you wanted that night you went with Raoul."

She gasped, trying to jerk out of his hold. What happened the night with Raoul was none of his business, and she told him as much.

"When I found out I wanted to destroy him. You were not my girl nor were you my daughter, but I wanted to tear his fucking head off."

Should she be delighted in what he said?

Licking her dry lips, she turned her head enough so she could see his face. His hands continued to hold her in place and tease her body. She'd never been this open with anyone, not even Raoul. That night she'd lost her virginity had been a disaster of the highest order. She hated it and would chose to forget it if she could.

"I've surprised you."

"Raoul's your brother. He's part of the club." While she was just a daughter, nothing special. She didn't add that last part.

"You're special. You just don't realize how fucking special you are." He moved his hand up her body, stroking over her nipple as he cupped her face. His touch ignited the arousal once again in her veins. "We keep this a secret only because you want to, baby. I don't. I want you, and I want the whole fucking world to know who you belong to."

"This is too much."

"No, baby. It's not enough for what I want to do with you. I can handle secret while you get used to the idea of being with me. Soon the club and people will know about us and you'll be by my side as my old lady."

"What about Julie?" She couldn't help but bring up his ex-wife. There wasn't a single comparison between her and Julie. Holly, she cared a lot about everyone. She loved taking care of the family and being there when they need it. She took after her mother in that regard. Julie cared about nothing and no one but herself. The other woman took selfish to a whole new level.

A lot of the time Holly was disgusted by the stuff she heard about Julie. Matthew, her son, didn't need her in his life. She was a bad influence and only served as a reminder to hurt him.

"Julie's a piece of shit who doesn't get anything. The only reason she's at my club is because of Matthew. You never have to worry about her." He pressed a tiny, fluttering kiss against her lips. Her heart raced at the contact.

"If I'm yours and I can't have another man, then neither can you."

"Baby, I've never been into dick." He chuckled.

"No more pussy, club or out of it. I don't share." She wouldn't spend her day worrying if her man was faithful to her. Holly refused to commit herself to an adulterer.

"I can handle that on one condition."

"You can't be throwing out conditions like this."

"We're secret and you don't want me to go to another pussy, then there's only one solution."

She was breathing harder as he pumped his fingers deeper into her core. Holly struggled to focus as he drove her to the edge of bliss but only teased her at what came next. He was the one in charge, not her. She loved the way he took charge. He made her believe nothing could tear them apart.

"What is it?"

"You. I like sex and fucking a lot. When I want it, you come to me. I call, text, or show up, you take my dick any way I want to give it." He smiled. "I see you like that. You're creaming against my fingers."

Holly bit into her lip trying to contain the moans.

"I want to hear those sweet moans, Holly. You better make sure I can hear every fucking thing."

He pinched her clit, and she released the scream she'd been holding back.

"What do you say, Holly? I'll be yours and you'll give me exclusive access to this body. If I want you to come to the club, you'll come, no questions asked. I call you to my house to strip and take my cock, you'll do it."

"Yes," she said, screaming out her agreement. Holly would do anything so long as he didn't stop touching her body. His touch was driving her crazy.

"Good girl. Now, come for me."

He stroked inside her pussy as he flicked her clit twice. She exploded into a searing hot orgasm that left her shaking. If it hadn't been for Duke holding her, she'd have collapsed in the stall of the shower. When her sanity returned sometime later and she was picking up the mess in the kitchen after Duke left, Holly hung her head.

What the hell had she agreed to?

Chapter Five

One day later Duke was flicking his phone backwards and forwards in his hand as he listened to Diaz break down the deal with the Mexicans. If the Trojans agreed to transport the coke from the shoreline through toward Vegas, a guy known as Ned Walker would deal with the distribution. The deal sounded neat, and they'd earn a cool three million in the year. It was a good sum, a dangerous sum.

"Ned Walker is responsible for the—"

"I know exactly who Ned Walker is, Diaz. I'm not a fucking moron. I know what goes down with other clubs and their businesses. I stay out of shit that's not my concern." Duke had known Ned, drank with the crazy old asshole. He had a lot of respect for the man who ran the Vegas Fighters. They were a mean bunch of bastards. It was hard to believe at times that a man so fucking mean could produce such a sweet girl. Duke remembered meeting Eva a long time ago before she split from the city. "Everyone knows The Skulls handle that shit. What the fuck is going on?"

Russ and Pike stood at his back while he sat with Diaz. They were in an abandoned warehouse outside of Vale Valley. This was neutral territory for them. His gun, along with the others weapons, was laid on a table a few feet away. This showed fucking trust for Diaz and the crew he kept. Diaz was neither part of an MC or an organization. He was the head of a street gang known as Diaz's crew, nothing more. Duke didn't give a fuck what the kid did providing he didn't bring shit into the town.

"The Skulls mostly deal with Walker. His daughter's screwing the president of the club, Tiny."

"I know what's going down. I'm not here to fucking gossip like teenage boys."

"Fine, sorry. The Skulls have dealt with a lot of heat the past couple of years. Walker's told the Mexicans to get new distributors. Skulls are pulling out for a while."

Duke couldn't blame them. That shit with Gonzalez was fucking nasty.

"What's the protection detail?"

"They've got several contacts in the local police force and pretty much anywhere that matters. They'll keep the heat off your back while you transfer the coke. The protection from possible intervention will come from yourself and your boys." Diaz nodded toward Pike and Russ. "We'll also be tailing you for your protection."

"I don't need you—"

"This is a lot of coke, a lot of money to be made. I've got a deal with Walker as well. We're going to be there to help ward off any attacks. I'm not here to take the deal off you. I'm here to make sure this shit goes through." Diaz's crew helped to deal the coke out to the locals in his town. "Control the shit, control the people, nothing bad happens."

"I'm going to need to vote on it with my crew."

"Take your time. You've got three days. The first shipment happens a week from Friday."

Nodding, Duke stood to his feet, shaking Diaz's hand. He pulled the little fucker close so that only they could hear what he was about to say. "You fuck with me on this, get any of my boys killed, or it comes back to my town, I will fucking kill you."

"It's not—"

"When I say kill you I'll make sure you're alive when I start removing body parts, Diaz. Don't fuck this up."

Diaz nodded. Duke respected the little shit as he didn't show any sign of being afraid. A man without fear was a dangerous person. They'd worked with Diaz a long time or at least Raoul had.

"I'll hear from you soon."

They all grabbed their guns, backing out of the warehouse as they each faced each other. No one turned their back on the enemy. Diaz was not club. He was part of a whole new crew. Once outside, Duke stared up at the beaming sun. It was hot, seriously hot, and all he wanted to do was sink into a nice warm cunt. Holly's warm cunt. She'd demanded him to be faithful, and she'd played right into his hands. Duke didn't cheat. He'd been faithful to Julie up until he caught her banging some other asshole.

While waiting for the divorce to come through, he'd fucked anything that walked. He and Julie had been long over. When they were still a couple, he'd looked at pussy, but he sure as fuck didn't taste any.

"What do you think of the deal?" Duke asked, pulling out a cigarette. He wouldn't call Holly for her ass to be at his place with her father in earshot. Duke had a lot more respect for Holly and for Russ.

"Sounds like a good deal," Pike said.

"A dangerous deal. We pulling coke with that profit for ourselves out of the books, you know it's ten times that amount."

"The money I don't give a shit about. We split it equally, and you know the score, no rash purchases or any shit that will show up on any fucking radar." Duke took a long inhale on his cigarette. "Shit with The Skulls is real. Talk says they're backing out for a while."

"Can't blame them," Russ said. "They've been through enough. Whatever you decide I'm on board with. I'm not president anymore, but that's why I picked you, Duke. You know to keep an eye on other clubs and to make the right decision for the Trojans."

"I'll do my best."

Russ straddled his bike. "I've got to get back. See you both back at the clubhouse."

Duke watched the older man leave. Flicking open his phone he dialed Holly's number. He'd gotten her cell number from her mother making the excuse it was for emergencies. She answered on the fifth ring.

"Hello," she said.

"Be at my place in two hours."

"Duke? How did you get this number?" she asked. In the background he heard the little kids she cared for at the local nursery making all kinds of noise.

"I've got my ways. My house, two hours, no panties." He closed the phone giving her no other choice but to comply. If she didn't, he was coming for her ass.

"Man, you've been flicking that phone backwards and forwards like it was a damn lifeline. You've been wanting to call Holly all day," Pike said.

"Breath a word of this to the boys—"

Pike held his hand up. "I'm not going to say shit and neither is anyone else. You've got the respect, but does she know all the boys know?"

"No. To her, we're a secret."

"And like the bastard you are, you're using it to your advantage."

"Holly, she's not like a lot of women I know. She'll run at the first chance she gets. What she doesn't realize is that I'm a damn good catch."

Pike laughed. "She's in for a lot of shocks."

"What about Mary? You heard about Mac at the diner?"

His friend paused, taking a long inhale on his cigarette before talking.

"Mac knows his place and what he's to do and not to do."

"You've ordered him to make a move on your woman?"

"I've told him to give Mary a chance as a possible partner in the diner. If she wants there to be more with him, fine. When the time is right, she's going to be mine. Until then, I want her to never have a moment's regret."

"Okay, that doesn't sound like you."

"It's not, but I've not got any choice."

"Why not?"

"When I take Mary, she's not getting away from me. I don't give a fuck what she says. Mary will be mine and all her regrets will mean shit."

Pike straddled his bike, turning the key in the ignition. Duke watched him, knowing Pike spoke the truth. He'd been the one who made sure Mary had a date to the prom. When Mary's father got a little fresh with his hands, hitting her, hurting her, it had been Pike to give the warning. From afar, Pike had cared about Mary. Duke even believed the one paying for her job was Pike. The diner hadn't needed any more waitressing staff, yet Pike made sure it happened.

"What are you going to do if she sticks by Mac?"

"She won't. I've made sure of it. Mac knows what to do."

Throwing his cigarette to the ground, Duke straddled his bike, following Pike out of the warehouse grounds. He knew the brothers would vote on the deal going ahead. They all had a nice stash of cash for retirement. Duke had put some of his in a trust fund for Matthew. The trust fund was in the name of his grandfather, who'd died over ten years ago. Since then, Duke had been adding to the account, only enough to show he wanted the best for his son. The other money he kept hidden in a safe at his ranch house. He didn't know how the other men dealt with their cash, but nothing had come back on them for the luxury.

When they got into Vale Valley, they both split up, Pike heading for the clubhouse and Duke toward his house. He had a date, and he wanted to be set up before she arrived. Matthew was still at school, and he had all afternoon to fuck his woman.

****

Holly paid the cab driver some money and climbed out the back. She didn't have a license, and walking was out of the question. Phoning her dad would be a big mistake, the worst mistake of her life.

Blowing out a breath, she saw the entrance to the house a few feet away. Duke lived in a private ranch with a large steel gate keeping everyone out. She'd pulled her hair into a tight ponytail, and she started to play with it as she walked. Her nerves increased with every step she took. Blowing out a breath, she looked left and right, expecting to see her father watching.

Get a grip.

Her shift had ended thirty minutes ago. Had he known? Would he have expected her to leave her job to come to him? In her bag she'd put the panties he'd demanded she not wear. The jeans she wore rubbed against her crotch as she walked, driving her crazy.

What are you doing?

She opened the gate and made her way inside. She took several deep breaths as she continued to walk. Mary didn't know what was going on between her and Duke. When Mary had finally made it back to their apartment last night, Holly had perfected the toffee, and lied about not having any visitors. She hated lying to her friend.

Within minutes she stood at the entrance of Duke's home. Stepping up the five steps, she walked to the door and knocked.

Before she finished, Duke opened the door. He wasn't wearing a shirt as he banded his arm around her waist, dragging her inside. She gasped. Duke slammed the door closed, pressing her up against the wall. His hand landed between her thighs.

"Where are your panties?" he asked.

"My backpack." Which she'd dropped outside.

He flicked open the button of her jeans, sliding his hand inside to cup her pussy. She cried out as he groaned. "You're already wet for me." He plunged two fingers inside her as he stroked his thumb across her clit.

She began to work her pussy on his fingers when he withdrew. Holly watched him lick her cream off his fingers.

"Take the jeans off."

Her hands were shaking as she worked the material down her thighs.

"Kick the boots off and step out of the jeans."

Holly wriggled out, and when she was finished she pushed them away from her. Duke reached out, grabbing her ass hard. "Turn around and grab your ankles."

She frowned but presented him with her back. Leaning forward, she grabbed her ankles, hating how open this made her. He'd see how big her butt actually was, and she hated that.

Calm down.

"All day I've been thinking about being inside you. I wondered if you'd be as wet as I imagined."

She groaned, closing her eyes.

The sound of his zipper and the clanking of his metal buckle were easily heard in the entrance hall of his house. Her heart raced as the belt seemed to caress over the cheeks of her ass.

He spread the cheeks of her ass wide, and she opened her eyes to see the wood floor in front of her. It was shining from a recent cleaning. She'd never been to Duke's ranch. Her first opportunity to be in his space and she couldn't even make it past the entrance hall.

"Have you been thinking about me?" Duke slid a finger into her pussy as he spoke.

When she didn't answer, he slapped the right cheek of her ass.

"Yes," she said, gasping at the sudden jolt of pain he created.

"When I speak, I expect an answer from you."

"Yes, I've been thinking about you." Last night she'd been thinking about him before she went to sleep. Then when she woke up, she was still thinking about him. She hadn't been able to stop thinking about him or what he was doing to her.

"When you're with me there will be no lies, Holly. I expect you to answer me honestly, and instantly."

She nodded. This man exceeded all of her expectations. Holly didn't know how any woman could have cheated on him. His mere presence took her breath away. The control he showed and exerted over her, made her want to give him everything. Her arousal had blown everything out of the water of what she felt before.

The tip of his cock slid against her entrance, replacing his fingers. She took a deep breath as he worked the head of his cock inside her. His hands returned to her hips, holding her in place as he slowly slid inside her. The width of his cock spread her open. She was aware of every inch as he stretched her open wide.

"Don't move your hands from your ankles."

Holly couldn't even if she wanted to. There was no sanity left. He was driving her crazy with wanting him, needing him. When only the last couple of inches remained, Holly screamed as he drove inside her in a hard thrust that left her gasping.

"That's it, baby. You've got all of me. Fuck. I can feel you squeezing me hard." He released a little growl that had all of her nerve endings answering his call.

Duke held onto her hips, tightly, pulling out of her only to slide back inside. He pumped into her pussy several times. Each time igniting the fire she had hoped would die once she got a taste of him.

"So fucking tight." He fucked her hard. Her hips already showed the bruises from his claiming yesterday. The way he held her let her know that there was no chance of her not bruising. His ownership would remain on her skin for as long as she stayed his woman. She didn't mind. Duke was showing a side of himself she didn't even think he was capable of.

"So fucking good and tight, baby." He slammed inside her going to the hilt, hitting her cervix. She cried out at the pleasure and pain mingled together. The sound of flesh hitting flesh was like sweet music to her ears, prolonging her pleasure.

Duke pulled out, cursing. "Stand up."

Holly did as he asked, gasping as he grabbed her arm roughly, leading her toward the stairs.

"Sit."

She spun around, sitting down. His cock stood out long, thick, and slick in front of her face. Without any instruction from him, Holly circled her fingers around the width of him, shocked by how big he actually was. He was coated in her cream, but she didn't mind. She took care of her body and knew she was clean.

Leaning forward, she licked the tip. Even with the musk of her own cum, she scented Duke mixed with her. The two of them together was a heady combination.

"Fuck, baby, have you ever sucked dick before?"

Holly shook her head. Duke's cock would be the first she tasted.

"Take the tip of me inside, go slowly, and enjoy the feel of me in your mouth."

She flicked her tongue across the tip, swallowing down his pre-cum before taking the whole head of his cock. Sucking her cheeks in, she lowered her mouth over his dick. Inch by glorious inch, she worked him inside until he hit the back of her throat. Before she gagged on his length, she pulled back, and released him.

"You don't need to stop. Keep your mouth on me."

Taking his cock into her mouth, she gazed up into his dark eyes. He wrapped her ponytail around his wrist, holding onto her head.

"Fuck, baby, if I had my phone right now I'd take a picture. Seeing your mouth open around my dick is fucking hot."

Thank God he didn't have a phone. She didn't know how she'd handle him taking pictures of them both together.

"Take more of me into your mouth."

She wrapped her fingers around the base of his cock, sucking his length into her mouth until she got to her hand. Moving back up, she didn't release him and worked up a pace that kept him in her mouth.

"Suck a little harder. Work your tongue around me."

Sliding her tongue around his length, she took more of him.

"You don't need to choke on me, baby. Gagging doesn't turn me on. Use your other hand to cup my balls." With his free hand, he guided her to his balls, cupping them together. She worked his balls between her fingers, listening to him moan. "That's it. Fuck, your mouth is perfect."

He was being way too nice. She knew it. This was her first time, but she'd take all the compliments she could take.

Duke guided her on how to suck, lick, and touch his dick. She followed his instruction, loving the feel of his width inside her mouth. He became her toy as she sucked his dick. With his hand in her hair, Duke set the pace, making her go faster or slower with his grip. She liked the little bursts of pain he created when he touched her.

Her own arousal was driving her crazy. She couldn't bring herself any release as she worked Duke's body with her hands. There wasn't a spare one for her.

"Fuck, baby, if you don't stop you're going to get a mouthful of my load."

Holly wasn't a fool. This may be her first blowjob but she knew what went on between a man and woman. In her mind the slender club whores passed through, each one looking more tempting than the other. They would swallow or at least make sure their man was taken care of.

For the next couple of weeks or until Duke got bored with her, he was hers. She wouldn't have him searching elsewhere.

Sucking harder on his cock, Holly was determined. Duke wouldn't look anywhere else.

"Holly, fuck, babe, you better stop."

She didn't pull away, nor did she let him try to ease her off his length when he tugged on her hair. Fighting the pain, she held onto him.

Within seconds he growled, his cock pulsed, and his cum filled her mouth. There was so much of it she didn't have a choice but to swallow. She milked his cock as he filled her with his cum, drinking every drop he spilled.

When it was over, she released his cock, resting her head against his thighs. They were both shaking. At least Duke had gotten his release. She was still waiting to find hers.

Chapter Six

Holly's hands rested on either side of his thighs as her head rested on him. Fuck, Duke couldn't remember a time he'd come so fucking fast from a woman blowing him. It had been Holly's first time. Her inexperience showed, but she'd listened to every single word he said, making it one of the best blowjobs he'd experienced. Duke had a lot of blowjobs under his belt. He liked having his cock sucked, but none of the other blowjobs had ever come close to being that amazing. Her mouth, the feel of her sucking him, it had all worked together to be phenomenal.

Never to be outdone, he sank to his knees, catching her hands in his and placing them above her head.

"Hold onto the stairs," he said, ordering.

"Duke, what are you doing?"

"You really think I'm going to let you suck my dick and not let you come yourself?" There's no way he'd let her out of his house without listening to her scream his name in orgasm. Opening her thighs, he moved in closer. Her pussy was bare and slick with her arousal. Cream coated her lips, and his mouth watered. She looked so tempting, so tasty.

He separated her lips with his fingers and leaned in close. Inhaling her musky scent, he let out a groan. Holly was shaking, and he'd barely touched her. It wouldn't take long to have her screaming in orgasm for him.

Sliding his tongue into her cunt, he felt her pussy ripple around him. She was so responsive and horny. He was surprised no other man had tried to snap her up. So many men let the good ones get away. Holly was a good one, better than good. She was a rare gem that men hoped to claim yet always failed. Women like Holly were always lost to men as they were too kind. They didn't demand attention when other women came flaunting their assets for men to see.

Duke wasn't like most men. He'd taken his time to get to know women. Over the years he'd been with a lot of women before he met Julie, then after her. He knew the women who only wanted the title of sleeping with him. Other women wanted to be by his side for his connections, and money. Some just wanted others to know they'd fucked a badass. Holly, she kept to herself, rarely letting anyone in. She was like a rare diamond, her body hidden away in jeans that she thought hid her round, curvy ass, and long shirts to hide away her large tits.

She spent a great deal of her life hidden away, working with her friend, only coming into the world when necessary.

He was going to open her mind in ways she never imagined. Trojans MC had a little tradition for their women. It was a tradition he never actually did for Julie. Did Holly know her own mother had gone through it, too?

Replacing his tongue with his fingers, Duke slid up to circle her clit. Glancing up, he saw her head thrown back in pleasure. Her whole body shook as he worked her pussy.

Each club had a different method of claiming women. Some clubs simply made a claim, married the bitch, and she was known as an old lady. In the Trojans, they made their possession known to the whole club. For a club whore to become the whore to the club, they were fucked in a room full of men, with each of them taking turns. Only when the club was satisfied with the bitch, she'd be taken into their protection with the description that they'd fuck any member, anytime, anywhere. Not all members had to fuck a club whore but enough had to. For an old lady to become part of the club, to be shown as a possession of the club, property almost, she had to be taken by her man in front of the club. No one was allowed to touch, speak, or interfere. They witnessed her becoming one at the hands of a member. From that moment on, she was protected. The club knew she was the old lady to that member, and that meant all hands were off.

The club respected the rules, and it had been happening for many years. When Russ asked him why he'd not taken Julie as his old lady, he'd not had an answer. Julie had been his old lady in name only, like their marriage. He couldn't bring himself to make such a claim with others watching. It wasn't just about the sex in front of the club.

Taking a woman, fucking her, making love to her, bringing her to orgasm for all the men to witness, took a lot of fucking guts to do. He was opening a part of himself up to the club, showing them his love of that woman.

When he took Holly, which he would, Russ wouldn't be present. Sheila's and Russ's parents were not present for their claiming of one another. The woman, in participating, also agreed to take care of the club as well to be loyal to their man. Duke would prepare her as his old lady soon. Until then, he was going to enjoy their time together when she thought it was only the two of them who knew.

Flicking her clit repeatedly, he relished her screams as he bought her to orgasm. Lapping up her cream, he groaned at the taste. He could lick her pussy all day every day.

"Beautiful," he said, pressing a kiss to her hip. Duke wiped the cum from his face.

"Thank you." She reached out to stroke his cheek.

"Come on, I've got something cooking." He took her hand, helping her to her feet. Duke pulled his jeans up and buttoned them up. Leaving his belt undone he led her through to his bedroom. The shirt she wore lowered down to mid-thigh. He'd have walking around naked, but he doubted she was ready to be that open with him.

"You cooked?"

He led her through to his kitchen, which was almost finished. The island had been finished last week, and all he needed to do was finish up the painting on the walls that hadn't been covered in cream tile.

"I can cook," he said. Opening the fridge, he pulled out a bottle of fresh orange juice and handed it to her. "Here."

She took the juice. "This place is nice. Who have you got decorating?"

Duke stared at her as she unscrewed the lid and glanced around. "I'm doing it."

"Really?" Her gaze returned to his, shock clear on her face.

"I'm good with my hands, Holly. I'm doing all the work. I've hired a plumber and electrician to do the jobs I can't do." He walked to the oven to check on the chicken he'd been baking.

It was done, and he pulled it out, snagging the bread that he'd put aside for the sandwiches.

"I know you're good with your hands. This place is amazing. Can you show me around?"

"It's not all done. I don't get to spend all that much time here." He worked at night while Matthew was doing his homework and went to bed.

"I'd still love a tour." She looked down at her lap, and he wondered what she was thinking. "This is the first time I've been here."

SAM CRESCENT

"You came by cab?"

"Yeah."

"Do you want the money?" he asked.

She frowned. "No, I don't want any money from you. I can afford a cab."

Staring at her, Duke waited for her to calm down before speaking. "I figured you didn't want people gossiping about me turning up to bring you back here. I'm happy to pay for your cab."

Holly licked her lips. "It's fine. I, erm, I wanted to come here anyway."

Slicing the chicken, he grabbed some lettuce, tomatoes, and cheese from the fridge. He'd already cooked the bacon earlier and arranged their sandwiches. Duke liked having her gaze on him, and he took his time in completing their food.

"Matthew in school?"

"Yeah, kid likes you."

"He's a good kid. You should be proud of him." She glanced toward the clock, and he looked over to see it was past two. Matthew would be coming home around five after basketball practice. Duke always picked him up from school after Julie fucked up.

"I'm very proud of him."

"He handling the life okay?"

"Better than I expected."

She smiled. "What did you expect?"

"Him acting out, becoming a bit of a prick 'cause his dad is president of the MC."

Holly chuckled.

"How did you handle it?"

"I didn't go off the deep end. Being the kid of a president isn't all it's cracked up to be. Matthew knows the loyalty of the club before you took over from my dad. I was told to act accordingly. My dad was president of the

71

Trojans, but I couldn't bring attention to the club. I was on good behavior."

"Bullshit, I bet Mary kept you out of trouble." He took a swallow of his orange juice as he smiled back at her.

"We kept each other out of trouble." She tapped her fingers together as she smiled at him.

He finished up their sandwiches, moving around the counter to present her with food. "I had no choice but to learn how to cook. Julie couldn't do shit in the kitchen. Matthew would have starved if I'd not."

"I like to cook."

Duke smiled. "You can come around one night if you'd like. Put those skills to good use."
****
Holly licked her lips. "Wouldn't that, erm, wouldn't that give the wrong message to Matthew?"

"No. We're friends, Holly. You'd be here as a friend. You'll stay the night, and I'll make sure you're out before he wakes up."

She nibbled her lip. It was already becoming complicated. One moment they were secret and now he wanted her to cook dinner.

You want to cook dinner.

"Okay." Holly liked being in his company. She didn't know what she'd say to Mary. The thought of lying to her friend twisted things deep in her gut.

Biting into the chicken sandwich, Holly moaned as the flavor exploded on her tongue. The chicken, cheese, bacon, and salad were so tasty and worked together.

"I take it you approve."

"Very." She took another mouthful not caring if he thought her a pig. Holly was so hungry, and she'd not eaten since breakfast. She missed lunch as one of the women at the nursery had gone down sick.

Within four bites she'd finished the whole sandwich, using the towel he offered to wipe her lips.

"I'm so sorry," she said, suddenly feeling like a pig.

Duke chuckled. "It's nice to see a woman appreciating her food. Besides, I'm fucking hot from seeing you eat that."

She groaned, pressing her hands to her face.

He finished his sandwich, and she stood beside him to wash the dishes. When they were done, she leaned against the counter, watching him move. She loved the sight of him naked. It was a shame he was wearing jeans as he had a nice ass.

"You want to see the house?"

She nodded. Her pussy was getting slick from watching him. He offered her a hand, which she took.

Duke took her out of the kitchen moving toward the dining room. The only furniture in the room was a sturdy oak table. "Did you make this?" she asked.

"Yes, how did you know?"

Running her fingers over the hard wood surface, she smiled at him. "Dad told me you did the table for church. He let me see it once when no one was inside the club."

"Russ let you in church?" He raised a brow at her.

"Only for a couple of minutes. He thought it was too good to not share." She'd been so impressed, and when she'd seen Duke without a shirt she couldn't help but wonder how good his hands would feel on her own body. She'd been so aroused that she couldn't look him in the eye at the time.

The room had pale cream walls.

"This was a rundown ranch, right?"

"Yeah, I had to re-plaster the walls when the electrician finished the wiring. Place had been left derelict." He leaned against one wall looking like the master of his domain.

The walls were plain apart from a couple of ink paintings on the wall. The room looked bare apart from the table.

"Are you, erm, going to make more furniture?" She imagined a dresser with nice porcelain along the wall underneath the painting.

"I've not had the time. I wanted to finish the decorating first." He took her hand once again leading her into the sitting room. The room was a dump. The walls showed signs of the re-plaster but no painting work. Boxes were stacked up on either side of the room with a sofa covered with a sheet. "I'm getting to this room."

"Would you like some help?" She could handle some decoration.

"Yes."

He tilted his head to the side as he looked at her.

"It would be a good reason for me to be here."

"It would. Do you really need a reason to be around me?" he asked. His fingers landed around her neck, and her heart started to race. His touch was possessive as he stroked over her pulse. He leaned in close, kissing her cheek. "You can never hide your response from me, baby."

She closed her eyes, gasping as he drew her back against his body. "Duke?"

"Don't think about it, Holly. Feel what I'm doing to you."

"I always feel what you're doing. That's the problem." She cried out when he pinched her nipple hard through her shirt.

"No, the problem is you thinking about everyone else when you're with me. I forbid it." He released her but kept hold of her hand. They made their way into the study. Books filled every bookshelf that he'd assembled. The room was half finished, and boxes were in the center of the room.

"You like to read?"

"Didn't expect that?"

She shook her head.

"You've been building up the cliché in your head when it comes to me?"

"Yes."

"You're a biker's daughter and yet you're making me out to be something I'm not. I've got another surprise for you, Holly. I finished high-school the top of my class."

"You were a nerd?"

"No. I just knew what I was doing." He kissed her head, leading her out of the study. Duke showed her the large pantry filled with food. "Matthew likes a lot of different food."

He led the way upstairs. The stairs was only partly finished. The banister had slats missing, and there wasn't any carpet on the stairs. The landing was also bare, but the floor showed signs of being treated and kept. The floor creaked as they moved.

The work he'd achieved was amazing. The artistry appeared in his work. The main landing was painted expertly along with all of the doors.

"I've completed two rooms and two bathrooms." He took her hand, leading her into Matthew's room. She was shocked to see three naked women posters on the wall. Duke laughed. "My son knows his own mind."

"He's a little young don't you think?"

"I lost my virginity at his age." Duke sounded proud of his son. "I doubt Matthew has had that pleasure, but I know he's getting ready for it." He opened a door, flicking on the light switch. "Walking in on your son masturbating gave him a bathroom all of his own."

Holly laughed. "Yeah, I like having my own bathroom. I walked in on my mom and dad. Scarred me for life." He laughed along with her. "What if it was your daughter?" she asked, changing the subject.

"What?"

"Her losing her virginity at fourteen, having naked pictures of men on the walls?"

The laughter on his face disappeared. "No daughter of mine will be touched by any fucker at that age."

"But you were happy about it for Matthew."

"It's different for men. It'll always be different. Any man or boy who put a finger on a daughter of mine will have to dig his own grave because I'll bury him."

She pressed a hand on his chest. "What are you going to do about my dad?"

"What?"

"If this gets out in the open what do you think he's going to do?"

Something came over Duke. She didn't know what it was, but it had her heart pounding inside her chest.

"Let's get something straight, Holly. You're over the age of consent, and you wouldn't be a quick fuck for me."

She tilted her head to the side, observing him like he'd done her. "What would I be?"

"You'd be mine. Your father would know you'd be my woman, my property, and you'd be taken care of."

Holly shouldn't be turned on by him calling her his property, but she was. Licking her suddenly dry lips, she tightened her hand within his grip. "Show me the other room you've finished." She knew it was going to be his room.

Did she really want him to lead her there?

The decision was taken out of her hand as he gripped her hand, taking her out of Matthew's room. He led her down the hall toward the last door on the right. Duke opened the door, stepping back to allow her inside.

His room had large French doors that opened up onto a small veranda. Her gaze was locked onto the safety of that escape. Duke didn't let go of her hand as she walked over to the doors. She opened one of the doors while he chuckled behind her.

"There's no escape out of there, baby."

Ignoring him, she stepped out into the warm sun. There was a large garden, and she saw a pool in the back of it. "Did you add the pool?"

"Yes, Matthew wouldn't move without a pool. He made a lot of requests before we moved. Little fucker was acting spoilt." Duke shrugged. "I couldn't blame him. I'd not long divorced his mother."

Close to the house she saw the basketball hoop, and she smiled thinking about that day at the clubhouse. "I bet Julie hates the fact she doesn't have a hold of this place."

"You're wrong. Julie would hate this place. She wanted me to buy a condo in the city, an expensive one, and go on a get rich quick scheme. The only thing she liked about the club life was the life, and easy sex."

He didn't sound angry.

"Do you wish you'd not married her?"

She turned around to look at him.

"The only reason I married the bitch was because she was pregnant. If she'd not had my kid growing inside her, she wouldn't have been in my life."

"If you hated her that much, why did you sleep with her?" For some strange reason she wasn't upset by his answer. There was clearly no love lost between the two.

"I was young, and any pussy would do. Julie was available and easy."

Holly figured as much. Her mother didn't like Julie.

Duke tugged on her hand, pulling her back into the bedroom. Her gaze landed on the large circular bed. She'd not expected him to have a circular bed. The size could easily fit four or more people on it.

"No one but me has slept in that bed," he said.

She glanced at him, seeing the sincerity on his face. "You don't owe me any explanation."

"I know, but I saw the look on your face. I've not brought a woman back to this place. I'm not going to lie to you, Holly. I've fucked women back at the club but never here."

She nodded, believing him. The room missed any feminine touch. Releasing his hand, she sat down on the bed, running her hands over the silk sheets. "You like the comforts in life."

"I do."

He stepped in front of her, pushing her back on the bed. Holly didn't fight him. She wanted this as much as he did. Spending time with him was making her life difficult as her feelings toward him were changing. In the past she'd been attracted to him. He'd been older, and his presence alone demanded her attention. She'd always been aware of him at the club, searching for him whenever she was present.

Even though she'd wanted him, been attracted to him, Holly knew there was no chance of ever getting him. Duke had access to all the club pussy available. Why would he even want her? Her own insecurity had led her into the arms of Raoul, the disastrous night she'd given him her virginity.

Duke grabbed one of her hands, pressing it against the side of her head. She stared up into his eyes. He reached between them, gripping his cock. Her breath hitched as he rubbed the tip through her slit. The ache started to build, and she spread her legs open even more.

"You're always so wet."

Not only did she have his attention, Duke wanted her back. She didn't know if he wanted her the same way she did him. Holly would take whatever he was willing to give her. When several inches were inside her, he captured her other hand, pressing it on the other side of her head. He slammed inside, fucking all of his length into her body. She bit into her lip, crying out at the explosive pleasure that consumed her body.

She couldn't keep fighting him. If she let down her guard it would only be a matter of time before she gave him a lot more of herself.

Closing her eyes, she arched up into his touch. He drove in and out of her body. She was so wet that even with his width, he thrust into her with ease.

"Eyes on me, Holly."

She opened her eyes and stared back at him. Neither of them spoke as he fucked her hard, forcing her to take the whole length. She wrapped her legs around his waist. His thrusts were relentless. Was he trying to make sure she wouldn't forget him?

He wasn't kind or gentle in his fucking, taking her harder than ever before. She splintered apart in his arms, climaxing on his thick shaft. His cock jerked within her, filling her once again with his cum.

When it was over, she lay on the bed panting for breath. Duke collapsed over. Their heavy breathing was the only sounds to be heard in the room. He held her to the bed with his cock still inside her.

It had only been a couple of days they'd been together physically, but she'd wanted him a lot longer. If she wasn't careful she was going to lose herself to this man, just like her mother had to her father. The very thought filled her with dread.

Chapter Seven

Duke waited outside of his son's high school for the bell to ring. He'd been standing for the last couple of minutes, but he didn't mind waiting. This evening Holly was going to be heading over to see him and help with some of the decoration. She still wanted to keep their relationship a secret, which was fine to him. His club knew to keep quiet, and they'd do what they were told. Club business was quiet at the moment. They'd all sat down and voted to take the Mexican deal, which Diaz was setting up. What Duke didn't like was news that Julie was hanging out with another gang, Dawg's— pronounced Dog—Crew, known for stealing women and selling them for a profit. Duke didn't mind dealing the drugs or selling guns, but what he hated was taking women against their will.

Most of the women on Dawg's books had been stolen or blackmailed in order for him to earn money off their backs. Duke didn't like it. If Julie was sniffing around that crew, it was bad business.

Trojans never mixed with Dawg. It was against their code. The club whores knew if they left the club and went with another man, they were out. There was no room for second chances.

It would only be a matter of time before he'd have to find out what the fuck was going on for Julie to be hanging around such a dangerous crew. Duke couldn't give a fuck what happened to her. He only cared about his son, Matthew.

Shit was getting serious with Holly even if she did want to keep them a secret. He didn't give a shit what she thought. She'd started to open herself up to him, talking about her life outside of the club. He'd already stopped by the Sheriff's office to give Deputy Phil a warning. No one sniffed around his woman, especially that piece of shit. She hadn't told Mary about them, but he knew it was only a matter of time.

Mary and Holly were close. When Mary found out, Duke would know Holly was ready to be open about their relationship.

The bell rang fifteen minutes later, and Duke watched the kids filing out of school. Several looked his way, and he stared right back at them. Their parents probably talked shit about the club anyway. Matthew came out alone. He held a piece of paper in his hand as he moved toward the parking lot. Duke decided on taking the car to pick up his son. He needed to talk to him about Holly.

"What are you doing here, Dad?" Matthew hitched his bag up his shoulder.

"Wanted to spend some time with my son."

"Mom changed her mind, didn't she?"

"No. I told her she wasn't having you tonight." It was a Friday night, and usually that meant Matthew would spend the night and Saturday with his mother. Julie hadn't put up a fight when he called. He couldn't believe he ever got her pregnant, but he loved Matthew and wouldn't change him for the world.

"Oh, okay."

"Actually, there's something I want to talk to you about."

"What?"

"Get in the car. We'll talk on the way home." Sliding behind the wheel, Duke waited for his son to climb into the car. He was tall and didn't have a lot of coordination. Firing up the car, Duke pulled away from the school, heading home. "Did you want to stay with your mom?"

"No, she's a bitch, Dad. She can't even stand me being there. I don't know why she even bothers arguing for the right to have me. She really doesn't like me." Matthew ran his hands up and down his thighs.

"Do you want to stop seeing her altogether?"

Matthew was silent for several minutes. Glancing toward him, Duke saw him staring out of the window. "Yeah."

"Yeah, what?"

"I want to stop seeing her altogether. I hate her. She doesn't want me around and spends most of her time asking questions about you."

Duke tensed up. "What do you tell her?"

"Nothing. When she really starts shouting, I tell her you're always decorating. She leaves me alone after that."

Matthew rubbed the back of his neck, looking uncomfortable. Duke decided to drop it.

"What did you want to talk to me about?"

"Holly."

He glanced over to see his son tense. "Russ's Holly?"

"Yeah."

"What about her?"

"She's going to be coming over this evening, and she offered to help me do some painting." When Matthew went to bed, he had a hell of a lot more plans for her than working.

"Cool."

"Do you like Holly?"

"She's cool."

Okay, Duke was sick to death of teenagers. "You like her, don't you?"

Matthew shifted in his seat.

He'd hit the nail right on the mark.

"I don't want to talk about this."

"I saw the way you were looking at her at the picnic a few weeks back. She talked to you."

"Holly's cool, and she's beautiful. I know some guys don't like women to be, I don't know, fat or whatever, but Holly's great."

Duke pulled into his home. He'd left the gate open when he went to pick up Matthew. "She's going to be my old lady."

He'd never kept anything from his boy before, and he wasn't going to start now.

"Aren't you a little old to be dating Holly?"

"You little shit. I'm not that old."

"She's what, six years older than me? What's to say she won't get bored of your ass?" Matthew was smiling, looking the happiest he had in weeks.

"Listen, you little shit, you keep your dirty little paws off her." He ruffled Matthew's hair, and his son slapped him back.

"Don't touch the hair."

"What? It's really great hair." He climbed out of the car. "So, you're fine with it?"

Even if Matthew wasn't fine with it, Duke wouldn't stop making Holly his.

"Is this like top secret?"

"It is. Holly's got a few hang-ups."

"I'm cool with it. Holly's cool."

He pointed at his son. "You better keep that crush buried tight, son. I won't have you drooling over my woman."

Matthew rolled his eyes. "Whatever."

Duke walked into his home, feeling contented. His son liked his woman. The first part was over, and now he just needed Holly to see they were going to be perfect together.

****

Holly glanced down at her cell phone to see a text from Duke blinking at her.

Duke: r u coming or what?

Holly: Be there soon!

Duke: U better. I've got a lot of plans.

Her pussy creamed at the sight of the texts. What were his plans? Every time he mentioned plans before they'd ended up having sex. Licking her suddenly dry lips, she lifted the cup to take a sip of the coffee. The cup shook a little spilling some of the coffee onto the table. She was waiting for Mary to get back from her shift in ten minutes.

Before she left for the night she intended to tell Mary the truth about what was going on between her and Duke. She nibbled her lip as she thought about what to tell her very best friend. The truth was the only choice.

Tapping her fingers on the table she growled in frustration as her cell phone buzzed once again.

Duke: Wear a skirt, no panties.

Holly: ur insane. I'm not wearing no panties and I'm not wearing a skirt.

She stared at her phone waiting for a response.

Duke: Wear a skirt, no panties.

Rolling her eyes, she dropped her phone to the table as the sound of Mary opening the door met her ears. Swallowing past the lump in her throat, she looked toward the kitchen doorway.

"Hey, Hols, you okay?" Mary said, walking straight to the kettle.

"I'm good."

"I'm so tired. I'm not going to be much company tonight. I've done nothing but double shifts the last week. I'm exhausted."

The kettle hadn't longed boiled, and within minutes she was sitting at the table opposite Holly.

"You need to stop working so hard."

"I like working."

Holly knew that was partly a lie. Mary loved working, but she hated working at the diner. The locals were not always friendly about Mary's drunk and drug addict parents.

When Mary clocked the overnight bag Holly had packed, she glanced from the bag toward her. "Are you going somewhere tonight?"

Letting go of her cup, Holly focused her attention on her best friend. "There's something I wanted to talk to you about." She stared into her friend's dark brown gaze. "I've not been completely honest with you."

"What about?"

"Duke, I've, erm, I've been seeing him." She expected to see anger in Mary's eyes, even upset at keeping her relationship a secret. What did she see? A smile. "Why are you smiling?"

"I've noticed you've been looking happier for the past couple of weeks. You're glowing but not in a pregnant woman way. I figured either Phil had stepped up his game or you were seeing someone and didn't want me to know." Mary reached across the table and placed her hand over Holly's. "Is it serious, or is it like a onetime thing?"

"It's serious. I think it's serious. I'm going over to his place tonight. My cab should be arriving very soon."

"Holly, I'm happy for you. Pissed that you were afraid to tell me but I'm happy for you." Mary got to her feet, moving toward her to pull her into a tight embrace. "I love you, Hols."

"I love you, too, Mary. What about Pike? Any news on him?"

"Pike's not for me. I'd never dream of ever approaching him, and he treats me like I don't even exist. I'd rather not go there at all if that's okay." Mary stepped back, rubbing her palms down her dress. Something wasn't right with her friend. Holly didn't know what.

"Is there something wrong?"

"No. Nothing, I'm fine. I mean, I'm tired all the time, but I'm fine."

"Is Mac getting a little fresh with you or something?" Holly asked, concerned for her friend's wellbeing.

Mary chuckled. "No. I'm fine. Please, go and have some fun."

Holly didn't want to leave her friend alone. "I'll call you when I get to Duke's house."

"Okay."

Nodding, she hugged her friend once more, grabbing her bag just as the sound of a car horn came. "That'll be my ride."

"Have fun."

She left the house, grabbing her cell phone as she scrolled through her contacts. Holly clicked on Pike's number, which Duke had given her in case of emergencies. She was starting to believe the whole club knew about them seeing as Daisy had been tailing her, Raoul stayed away from her, and she had half of the guys' cell phone numbers programmed into her phone.

"What?" Pike asked.

"Hey, that's no way to answer the phone."

"Tell me what you want, Holly. I've not got all day."

"Fine. I'm worried about Mary." Silence met her words. "I was wondering if there was anything you knew about that?"

"What do you mean?"

"I don't know. She just seems withdrawn. She's not herself, and I don't like it."

"Where is she?" Pike asked.

Holly nibbled her lip. Should she tell him Mary was alone?

You're going to be out of your apartment all night. Tell him.

"She's back at our place. I'm going out for the evening."

Pike cursed. "I'll deal with it."

Before she could say anymore he hung up. Cursing, she pocketed her phone and wondered if she'd done the right thing in calling him.

Chapter Eight

Duke stared at Holly's rounded ass while she pulled out the chicken bake she'd put in the oven an hour ago. They'd all been working in the sitting room, painting up the walls, while he put together furniture with Matthew. While she painted with a roller, she gave Matthew a spelling test that he needed for English along with a pop quiz for biology. His son was fast at answering all the questions, only getting a few wrong.

They'd taken a break. They were alone, and he needed to kiss her. She'd been talking about Mary. He'd gotten a message from Pike to say he was handling Mary. Duke didn't want Holly worried or thinking about her friend when she was with him. He'd make sure everything was taken care of.

There wouldn't be any room for complications in their life.

"Okay, that just needs to rest before we burn ourselves." The moment she removed the oven gloves she'd put on, stepping back from the steaming hot food, Duke wrapped his arms around her. Pulling her close, he gripped her hips as he rubbed his cock against her ass.

"I've been wanting to do that all night."

He heard her sigh, leaning back. "You've got to stop."

"We're alone, and you didn't wear a skirt. I'm going to take care of that later." He breathed in the scent of her neck. Flicking his tongue against her pulse, he slid one hand down to cup her pussy. "Are you wet for me?"

"Yes."

There wasn't a hesitation in her response. She gave to him, and he relished it like a starving man needing food. He slid his hand into her jeans finding her wet heat. She was soaking wet.

"Why didn't you wear a skirt?"

"I didn't know how much bending I was going to do. I won't flash my personals at your son." She tilted her head back far enough for him to see her eyes. They were dilated, filled with arousal and heat. She captivated him in ways he couldn't even begin to understand.

"Fine, I won't punish you so much, but you've got to give me this."

He teased her clit, stroking his fingers across her nub, listening to her moan. She shook in his arms. Holding her still, he sucked on her neck at the same time. When she was in his bed tonight, he intended to fuck her all night long. He was going to have her screaming out his name. Duke wanted her to watch as he fucked her hard, claimed her.

"I want you to come for me, to scream my name as you give yourself to me." He reached down, plunging two fingers inside her, loving the way she moved on his hand. She was as wanton as he was. Flicking her clit with his thumb, he brought her face close to his. Slanting his lips over hers, he took the kiss he'd been craving from the first moment he saw her that night.

"Please," she said, breaking away from the kiss long enough to whisper the words.

Licking her lips, he teased her clit, pinching the little bud. "Come for me, Holly."

He plunged his tongue into her mouth, and pressed her clit hard, which was all it took. Duke held her close as she splintered apart. He swallowed her screams so no one but him knew the kind of pleasure she was getting. When it was over, he pulled his hand out of her jeans, sucking off her cream. "Delicious."

"Hey, guys," Matthew said.

Holly pulled out of his arms so fast it was hard for Duke to contain his laughter.

"Dinner's ready." She put on the gloves again and carried the casserole through to the dining room. He sat at the head of the table with his woman one side, his kid the other. Duke couldn't remember a time when he'd done this with Julie. All he recalled from his married days was the arguing, screaming, cursing, and shit. This was real.

Holly pulled Matthew into a conversation, getting him to come out of his shell. Duke joined in, helping the two to get along. Afterwards they all did the dishes before going back to decorating.

Matthew put on some music that Duke hated. It was pop, but he soon patted his son on the back as Holly sang along to the music, dancing, and shaking her fine ass. Each time she stopped to look at him, he made her aware of the dirty thoughts running through his mind. He was going to fuck her very soon, have her screaming out in pleasure.

By the time Matthew went to bed, the sitting room was completed. Holly held the paint bucket in her hand, staring at what they achieved. "We did good."

"I've got to pick out a sofa, couple of chairs, and this will be complete." He wrapped his arm across her shoulders, admiring their work. "Come on, it's time for bed." Duke took the bucket out of her hand, putting it to the floor. She released a squeal as he hauled her up into his arms.

"What are you doing? Let me go."

He put her over his shoulder, slapping her ass as he made his way upstairs. "I'm taking your fine ass upstairs to punish you."

"Why are you punishing me? I've done nothing wrong."

Duke kicked open the door to his room, dumping Holly on the bed as he kicked the door closed, locking it.

"I seem to recall a certain text that told you to wear a skirt."

She rolled her eyes at him. "I told you why."

"I don't care. I gave you an instruction, and now you're going to pay the price." He advanced to the bed. Holly didn't pull away. She stared right back at him on her knees. Reaching out, he gripped her hips, flipping her onto her knees.

"What are you doing?"

He held her around the waist, smoothing his hand across her ass. Raising his hand, he brought it down hard on her ass. She squealed, trying to fight him.

"Get off me."

Duke brought his hand down three more times, slapping her ass. On the last spank, he released her but not for long as he grabbed her jeans. She was laughing by the time he got her jeans down her thighs.

"You're insane."

He didn't speak, using all of his time to get her naked. Stepping away from the bed, he tugged his shirt over his head, releasing his jeans. When he stood before her naked, he worked his cock, which was already rock hard.

"You spanked me!"

"And you liked it." She deserved it, too. He'd wanted her to wear a skirt so that he'd get a peek of her pretty pussy. "Open your legs."

She sat on the end of the bed, looking so damn tempting. Holly raised a brow and slowly eased her legs open.

Closing the distance, he presented the tip of his cock to her waiting lips. "Taste me."

Holly took him between her lips, moaning as she licked every inch of his rock hard cock.

"You're so fucking beautiful. Take more of me." He sank his hands into her blonde tresses. Wrapping the strands around his fist, he thrust his hips, plunging his dick deep into her mouth.

"Fuck, yeah, baby, so fucking beautiful."

Looking to his right, Duke almost came in her mouth. The floor to ceiling mirror showed her taking his dick. Each time she withdrew meant his cock, covered in her saliva, was visible.

Pulling out of her mouth, he pulled her off the bed, turning her to face the mirror. Look at yourself, baby."

Holly stared at her reflection. She tried to pull out of his arms.

"No, you're not moving."

"Duke, please, I really don't want this."

Holding her in place with a hand on her stomach, he glided down to cup her bare pussy. "I want you to see what I see." Delving his fingers into her core, he worked her pussy like he had down in the kitchen.

Her gaze focused on him. Seconds passed before she wrapped her fingers around his cock. "If you get to touch then so do I."

He wasn't going to argue.

****

This was dangerous. What was happening between them was dangerous. Holly needed to take a step back yet she felt herself getting drawn back toward him. Why couldn't she walk away? Spending the evening with him and his son, now she was going to be sleeping beside him, what the hell was happening?

The club life wouldn't be for her. Phil came around to the nursery, and she'd gently let him down. He didn't look all that concerned for them to no longer be dating.

"What's going on in that head of yours?" Duke asked, kissing her neck.

He created a fire inside her that she was terrified of becoming trapped inside. She licked her lips, running her thumb over the tiny slit of his cock, coating it with his cum.

"Nothing."

"Don't lie to me. You don't get to fucking hide from me, Holly." The hand on her waist traveled up her body until he cupped her around the neck. He wasn't hurting her, only letting her know his strength.

She turned her head to look at him.

"Tell me."

"This is too much."

"What's too much?" He continued to play with her pussy, and she struggled to fight the burning need.

"This, between us. I can't handle this. It's only supposed to be fun."

His gaze darkened, but he didn't stop touching her. Duke dropped a kiss to her cheek. "I've got news for you, Holly, this isn't about fun. I want you. I've waited a long time to take you, and you're not getting away from me."

She'd heard him say all that before. Holly tried to fight him. Duke overpowered her, pressing her up against the wall. He grabbed her hands, trapping them above her head, stopping her from moving.

"No, you're not going to fight me, and you're not going to run."

Fear clawed at her. The fear wasn't of Duke or his strength. She knew more than anything he'd never hurt her, wouldn't even try to. No, the fear came from the unknown. She'd never given herself to a man before, not emotionally. Physically she'd given herself to Raoul, but she'd not really done so then. With Duke, he broke down the walls she'd spent a great deal of time erecting. He was making her feel for him. The crush she'd had growing up had turned into something more, something frightening and painful.

"I can't do this." Tears filled her eyes.

Stop it, Holly. This is only supposed to be fun.

She couldn't fight the emotion clawing at her. No matter how far she ran Duke would follow. There was no getting away from what was going on between them.

"You're doing this." He stroked her cheek. "I'm about to say something to you that I've never said to another woman."

Holly took a deep breath, scared, excited, nervous—it was all there crashing together, threatening to spill over.

"I love you."

"You can't know that." Tears she'd kept at bay finally spilled over. No man had ever told her that they loved her. Could she believe him? Should she believe what he had to say?

He's never lied to me.

"I know that. I also know that you wanted me back when you were eighteen, but I was married. When you came to the clubhouse, you'd look for me. You were always looking for me."

Her breathing deepened. "You knew?"

She'd done everything to keep her attraction at bay.

"I knew, and I fucking hated it. You were so fucking young. I kept telling myself I'd wait, give you time. Then Raoul came into the picture. I wanted to tear him apart. He took what was mine, what was always supposed to be mine."

This was raw. What he said she always dreamed of listening to.

"You were mine, Holly. This is about way more than getting my rocks off. You're real to me."

"What are you trying to say?" she asked, almost afraid of what he was going to say.

He stroked her cheek. Both of his hands cupped her cheeks, holding her in place. "You know what I'm trying to say, but I'm going to tell you anyway."

She took in a deep breath waiting for him to speak.

"I love you, Holly Crock."

More tears filled her eyes as she stared back at him.

"You love me."

"You bet your ass that I do. I love you. I've never told another woman that I love her. When I knew what I was feeling for you I was terrified. You were a fucking teenager. I did everything I could to stay away from you. Then that shit happened with Raoul, and I just knew it wasn't him you wanted. I got so fucking angry. You're mine. You've always been mine."

"Yes. I've always been yours." There was no use denying it. She'd wanted Duke, but when he was married she refused to even consider a life with him.

He leaned in close pressing a kiss to her lips. "You're going to by my old lady. No one at the club is ever going to show you any disrespect."

"What about Raoul?"

"He'll keep his mouth fucking shut."

"Okay." She couldn't stand for the other man to ruin what happiness she had with Duke.

"I promise. I'll talk to him."

Holly ran her hands up his chest. His muscles rippled beneath her touch. Glancing down she couldn't resist. She pulled out of his hands, moving down to circle one of his nipples. Licking across his chest, she took his other nipple between her teeth, moaning.

He ran his hands through her hair, not holding her in place, simply holding her. Holly loved his touch more than anything.

Within seconds, he gripped her arms, moving her over to the bed. Placing her on the bed, he followed her down, sliding between her thighs as he did. He gripped her hands, and he locked their fingers together on either side of her head.

Duke moved his hips until the tip of his cock moved against her entrance. She stared up into his eyes, waiting for him to let her go. He didn't need to let her go. Duke was that hard and thick, and she was so wet that he eased inside her without any barriers between them. Not once had she asked him if he was clean.

"What?" he asked.

She'd spoken out loud. "Are you clean? I've never asked you."

"Baby, I wouldn't be fucking you without a rubber if I wasn't clean." He dropped a kiss to her lips, licking her bottom lip before he plunged inside her. She moaned, opening up to him, loving the feel of his mouth on hers.

He thrust inside her. His cock went so deep with that one plunge. Wrapping her thighs around his waist, she stared into his eyes, needing him to surround her with his warmth.

"I'm never going to let you get away from me. No man is going to look at you. You're going to be all mine."

"Yes."

He rammed inside her. There was no steady pace to his possession. Duke fucked her hard while keeping her in place on the bed. She met each of his thrusts, taking the passion he wanted to give her. When she made to cry out, he swallowed her screams in kisses. He swiveled his hips, creating the most wonderful friction against her clit.

She went up in flames, and Duke with three more thrusts followed her back into bliss. They collapsed over each other. Duke stayed inside her, stroking her face, loving her. For the first time in her life she felt complete in his arms.

"I love you," she said, no longer embarrassed by the extent of her feelings for this man.

"Do you still want to keep us a secret?"

Holly smiled, shaking her head. "No, I don't want to keep us a secret. It was silly to have done so anyway. The club knew, didn't they?"

He stared at her without answering.

"Not all women get each club member's number in their cell phone. You took my cell and added them all, didn't you?"

"They know, but they won't say anything until you're ready."

"I want to tell my dad first. It's important."

"We'll wait for the rest of the club to know until you're ready. I'm not going to force you to do anything you don't want to do." He caressed her face with his nose. She loved the attention, basked in it.

"Thank you."

She couldn't wait to tell Mary. Her life was finally coming together. Duke was her man, and she looked forward to being his woman. She'd tried to get away from the biker lifestyle, but she should have known there was no chance. The man who owned her heart was the president of the club. She'd stand by him no matter what.

Chapter Nine

Duke woke up to Holly climbing over the bed. She was trying to be quiet. Glancing over at the clock he saw it was five in the morning. They'd only fallen asleep a couple of hours ago.

"What the fuck are you doing?" he asked, groaning. Running a hand down his face, he really wanted to go back to sleep. He was exhausted. Holly had kept him up half the night demanding that he fuck her. They'd not been together for a long time, and she was more than making up for it now.

"It's early. I've got to go."

"Fuck, Hols, it's five in the morning. My son already knows about us."

"I don't want him to know about us yet. He's got a mother. Do you really want him to run back to Julie?"

"Matthew wouldn't do that. He's a good kid."

"I'm not saying he's a bad kid. Shit, I don't even know what I'm saying anymore. Ignore me."

He chuckled. "You're nervous."

"Hell yeah. Why wouldn't I be?"

"You've got nothing to be nervous about. I promise."

She pressed her hands to her face. "I'd like to wait until I've spoken to my parents."

Duke released a sigh. There really was nothing he could do. She looked so damn nervous and cute. He liked her cute. Running his thumb along the back of her cheek, he smiled. "That's your call. When you're ready to handle us in front of everyone then we'll handle it together."

Any other time he'd have taken the decision out of her hands, but Holly wasn't like most women. She'd been hurt before. He wouldn't be responsible for hurting her again.

"Thank you." She leaned forward, brushing her lips against his. "I'll get dressed. Are you good to give me a ride home?"

"Sure."

He watched her climb out of the bed, naked. Duke didn't move, admiring her ass as she bent over to retrieve a shirt out of the bag. She looked so damn sexy. Her blonde tresses cascaded down, and her breasts looked so tempting. The tips were nicely bruised from his lips.

Holly disappeared into the bathroom. She'd need to get used to dressing in front of him. Pushing the covers back, he climbed out of bed, heading toward the closet. He was dressed within thirty seconds in a pair of jeans and plain white shirt. She came out of the bathroom with her hair bound up, exposing the long line of her throat.

"I've just thought. You can't take me home. I can't ask you to leave Matthew here on his own." Closing the distance between them, he cupped her face.

"My son would go fucking crazy if he thought you'd risk your safety because he needed a babysitter. Trust me. He can stay home for a couple of minutes on his own. I'll lock the place up."

She pressed a hand to her head. "Sorry. I completely forget at times that he's, you know, a teenager."

Duke nodded, taking her hand. She had her bag over her shoulder.

"Come on."

He didn't want her to leave but knew he wouldn't have much of a choice. "Okay, let's head out."

Together they made their way to his car. There wasn't a chance in hell of him taking her back on the motorbike. The mornings were warm, but he wanted her to be comfortable before riding on the back of his bike, which was something she hadn't done.

Pulling up outside of her house, he climbed out of the car, walking her to the door. "You didn't have to follow me."

"My woman, my rules." He caught her face in his hands, slamming his lips down on hers. "I expect to see you tonight. It's Saturday."

"Don't you usually party at the club?"

"Not tonight."

"Okay." She kissed him one final time. He waited until he heard the lock click back into place in the apartment before heading back to his car. Climbing behind the wheel, he headed back. It was past six by the time he got back to the house, and he saw the light on in the kitchen.

He found Matthew sitting, eating cereal, and playing a video game.

"She did know that I wouldn't say shit, right?"

"Holly's delicate. If you're fucking up I may as well get shit done." He headed for the coffee machine, groaning when he saw it was empty. "What are you doing up?"

"I'm always up this early."

Duke glared across at his son and started muttering about early risers. "I'm heading into the garage."

"Sure."

Leaving the kitchen, he went to his workshop where he was fixing up some more bookcases. He liked to make everything himself. Duke trusted his own craftsmanship while he detested the faulty goods people like to buy from the store. By the time ten came he got a text from Holly letting him know she was heading over to her folks'. She also asked what Pike had done to Mary.

Duke: Mary?
Holly: She's withdrawn and looks strange.

"Dad, Pike, Daisy, and Raoul are here," Matthew said, shouting for him to hear.

Staring at the bookcase, he put down his tools, and headed out to greet his men.

He shook Pike's hand along with Daisy's. Like all the other times before he gave Raoul a nod of the head. He didn't like the fucker, and if it was up to him the bastard would have been voted out years ago. Raoul had contacts that were vital to the club.

"What's going on?" he asked.

"Diaz called. Our first shipment deal is this coming Friday. We're to drive it straight through to Ned. He'll handle the coke from there. First payment comes from collection, second payment, delivery," Raoul said.

"Okay, sounds like a done deal. All the boys in?"

"Yeah, Knuckles isn't too happy. He's on guard duty while we're gone. Russ is also staying back to keep an eye on shit," Daisy said.

Duke nodded. They all took it in turns on long rides for one of them to stay home. Duke no longer got a choice about staying home. As club president, he went on each delivery.

"Why does it take three of you to head out here?" he asked.

All three of his men looked at each other.

"Spit it out. I can't be done with this playground shit."

"Julie's at the club. She's high and demanding to know what whore you're banging in front of her son."

Duke's temper rose. "What the fuck's she doing in the club?"

"Mandy let her in."

Gritting his teeth he stared toward the house. Mandy was a club whore and a pretty popular one. "One of you stays here. The other two come with me. Raoul, you're on babysitting duty."

The brother didn't argue and headed toward the house. "What the fuck is going on with you and Mary?" Duke asked.

"No offence, Prez, not your business."

Duke stopped beside his bike. "When it affects my woman, it becomes my business. Don't make it become my business."

"Fine."

Straddling his bike, he followed Pike and Daisy toward the clubhouse. The sun was shining, and the town of Vale Valley looked more beautiful than ever before. He loved living in this town that was on the edge of a city. They were close enough to the local malls but far enough away that they were left alone. Most people stopped by for gas on the way out of the city. The small town thrived with several ranches on the outskirts. If he'd not been president of the Trojans, Duke imagined he'd have turned his ranch back into a cattle one. He knew next to nothing about cows, sheep, or pigs. There was no way he was passing in his cut for a chance to find out.

By the time he got to the clubhouse he heard Julie shouting from the outside. Several brothers were standing, smoking cigarettes as he made his way inside. Across the grounds he saw Junior working on the cars while several of the other workers stood back watching him. "What the fuck do I pay you for? Get back to fucking work."

Entering the clubhouse he found Julie with a smashed bottle in her hand, pointing it at his men, screaming at them. From the look in her eyes, he knew she'd taken some weird shit.

"Julie, what the fuck are you doing?" he asked.

This woman was the thorn in his side. He fucking hated her, despised her. The only saving grace she had was the fact she was Matthew's mother. Otherwise he'd have killed the bitch long ago.

"You think of replacing me?"

"What the fuck?" he asked, stepping closer. She kept the bottle raised, glaring at him.

Folding his arms over his chest, Duke watched her, waiting. "I take it you've got something to fucking say. Go ahead, I'm listening to whatever shit you're going to tell me."

"You took Matthew. You've got another woman. I know you have."

"So what the fuck if I have?" he asked, glaring at her. Julie was hanging on by a fucking thread, and if she crossed the line Duke would see her six feet under. "Put the damn bottle down."

Her hand shook.

"You think I don't know about Dawg's Crew and your little visits to them?" he asked. "You should be fucking lucky you're not dead right now."

She threw the bottle down to the ground. Grabbing her arm, he tugged her into the room they had church in. He was pissed, shaking with anger that she'd fucking threaten him. Pressing her into a chair, he glared at her, waiting for himself to calm down.

"I'm your woman, Duke."

"No, you're not. You've not been my woman in a long fucking time." He glared at her, hoping she'd shut the fuck up. "You've never been my woman, Julie. The only luck you ever fucking had was getting knocked up by me."

Gripping the arms of the chair, he pressed his face against hers.

"Who is she?" Julie asked. She started to scratch her arms.

"What the fuck are you doing to yourself?" He didn't care, but the sight of her sickened him. Duke didn't know how he could have stooped so low as to be with her.

"Me, what about you? Who is the whore?" She spat the words at him. He reached out, catching her jaw in his hand.

"Let's get something straight, you don't get to call her a whore or to talk about her."

"You can't keep her a secret forever. She's part of the club, isn't she?" Julie glared at her.

"How did you know?"

"Dawg's Crew has resources. He let me know exactly what you've got going on."

Duke gritted his teeth. They all had their resources, but he didn't know how Dawg could have found out about Holly.

He hasn't. He only knows you're seeing someone.

"It's Holly, isn't it? I saw the way you looked her on the Fourth of July celebrations. You've always been panting for her. She's eighteen years younger than you, you fucking perv."

He grabbed her arms, slamming her against the wall. Duke wrapped his fingers around her neck, squeezing tight.

"Let's get something straight, you fucking whore. Holly is no business of yours. You'll stay out of my club, my business, and if you so much as come near her, you're fucking dead."

Duke released his hold around her neck.

"You wouldn't kill me. I'm the mother to your only son." She smiled at him, looking like she'd won some great battle.

He smiled, but there was no laughter in his eyes. Duke saw the smile on her face disappear. She'd fucked up.

"You've not got a leg to stand on, Julie. Our son hates your guts. You're on borrowed time." He pulled away from her. "Get the fuck out of my club, now!" He yelled the last word.

She ran away.

Daisy came to stand beside him where he was standing in the doorway.

"Put protection on Holly."

"If you don't trust her, why is she walking out of here?" Daisy asked.

"I've got to know who's watching us. When I do, unless Matthew says otherwise, she's going to find a nice eternal sleep."

****

"Mary, are you okay?" Holly asked. Their apartment looked the same as always apart from the fact Mary was wrapped up in a blanket on the sofa. This was how Holly had found her friend when she walked into the room. She'd not thought to go after Duke to ask him what was going on.

"I'll be fine." Mary took the mug of coffee from her. Sitting on the sofa beside her friend, Holly stared at her.

"I'm worried about you. You're not one to camp out on the sitting room. What about work?"

"I'm, erm, I'm going in a couple of hours." Mary had tears in her eyes.

"Tell me what happened." She took Mary's hand in her own.

"I know you called Pike. I, we, erm, we had sex." From the look in Mary's eyes, Holly's gut twisted.

"It wasn't good?"

"It was nice. I mean, I thought it was nice. I don't know. Could we not talk about it?" Mary sipped at her drink.

"I'm completely confused right now. You've got a thing for Pike."

"And he proved to me why it could never work." Mary's smile was watery. "Please, Holly. I know why you called him and I understand, but it's done. Whatever happened between Pike and me ended last night." Mary gripped her hand. "Some things are just not meant to be."

Holly tightened her hand around her friend's.

"Tell me what happened with you and Duke."

"I can't."

"You're happy. Please, I've woken up after being asleep for so long when it comes to Pike. It'll never work. Tell me about your time with Duke."

Holly let out a sigh. There wasn't a chance of getting Mary to open up to her.

"He told me he loved me."

Mary squealed, wrapping her arms around her. "I'm so happy. I've always told you Duke has got a thing for you."

For the next hour Holly told Mary every little detail of her time with Duke, not leaving anything out. She saw the blush staining her friend's face.

"Wow, he sounds so dreamy."

"I've got to head to my parents'. I want to tell my dad before I head to the clubhouse."

"Are you spending some time with Duke later?"

"I was going to. What do you have planned for tonight?" Holly asked. Her friend's wellbeing came first.

"I've got another double shift. It's fine. I'm going to work, come home, take a shower, and then bed."

"I hate leaving you."

Mary stood up, wrapping the blanket around her. "You're not leaving me, Hols. I've got work. Go, see your dad."

Nodding, Holly got to her feet. "I'm going to head out."

"See you soon." She watched Mary walk away toward her own room.

Grabbing her bag, she dialed the number for a cab. She took their cups into the kitchen as she went.

Holly: What did u do to Mary?

Pike: Not ur business.

Holly: She's my friend.

Pike: Then u shouldn't have called me last night.

Tapping her foot, Holly glared at her phone. What the hell was going on between the two?

Shaking her head, she headed out of the apartment calling goodbye to Mary. When Mary shouted one back to her, Holly closed the door behind her. The cab was waiting. She gave him the address, and she sent a quick text to Duke.

Duke: It's their business, baby.

She released a sigh, sitting back in her chair. Folding her arms underneath her breasts, she stared out of the window. The driver didn't try to make more conversation, which she was thankful for. She really wasn't in a talking mood right now.

She paid him as she climbed out of the car. Her parents' house held a great deal of mixed memories for her. She remembered when her father had bought the place years ago. She'd been six years old, and before they moved here, they'd lived in a one bedroom apartment. Life had been uncomfortable for the longest time.

Russ was putting out the trash as she entered the garden.

"Hey, Dad."

"Honey." He pushed the bag into the trash, walking over to her. She was pulled into his bear hug a second later. Giggling, she held him close. "I've missed you around here, honey."

She smiled, pulling away. "I've missed you, too."

Glancing up toward the front door she saw Sheila standing with a towel in her hand. "I made breakfast, Holly. Come on inside."

"Why do I get the feeling this is not a social visit?" Russ said. They made their way up to the house together.

"It is and it isn't." She put her purse down on the door, kicking off her sneakers to head toward the kitchen.

The scent of baked bread met her senses.

Sheila was cutting up some bread. Three places were set at the dining table with breakfast already waiting. "Go and eat."

Sitting on one side of her father, she waited for her mother to take a seat before she started to eat.

"What brings you out here?" Russ asked, biting into a chunk of bread.

Heat filled her cheeks as she thought about Duke. How did she tell them she was seeing him? She felt put on the spot just by talking with her folks.

"Erm, I'm seeing someone." She gazed down at her plate. Her hands were shaking.

"Do we know him?" Sheila asked.

"Yeah, you both know him."

Russ reached across the table. "Honey, we know."

Her shoulders sagged.

"Just say the name," Russ said.

"I'm seeing Duke Bana." She forced herself to look up at her parents. Sheila and Russ shared a look before turning back to her. "What's with the look?"

"You've had a crush on him for the longest time," Sheila said.

Her cheeks went from warm to burning hot. "Mom, please." Here she was thinking she'd hidden her crush well.

"What, honey? It wasn't a secret. Well, maybe it was a bit of a secret, I don't know." Sheila tapped her hand. "I'm happy for you."

Holly looked toward her dad. Russ hadn't said anything else since she started to talk.

"Dad?"

"I'm not going to lie, honey. I don't like the fact he's older than you. In fact, I want to fucking castrate the bastard, but I know he cares about you. He wanted to ruin Raoul. I knew then something was going on between the two of you. Your mother filled in the other blanks."

"Are you happy about it?" She nibbled her lip, shocked by how much she wanted them both to be happy with her decision to be with Duke.

"Holly, if I didn't like Duke he wouldn't be running the club. He's a good man. No man will ever be good enough for my daughter, but I'm happy for you both. I know he'll never make the mistakes that I made." Her father reached out to take her mother's hand.

"You know we've had our difficulties, Holly. Your father and I, we got through it. We're strong together." Sheila smiled, going red as Russ leaned over, sucking on her neck.

"Like I said, I was an asshole, and I paid the price for my sins. You've got nothing to fear with Duke. He's a damn fine man."

From her father that was a good start. Getting to her feet, she went behind him, wrapping her arms around his neck. "I love you, Daddy."

"I've come to see something else," he said. "It's 'Daddy' whenever you get what you want or if you want something and you need me to get it for you."

Sheila laughed, and Holly joined her.

"He wants me to be his old lady," she said, taking a seat.

Glancing up she saw Sheila and Russ share a look. "What is it? What's wrong?"

"You better make sure he warns her," Sheila said, getting to her feet.

"I will." Russ turned his attention back to her. "Nothing to worry about. I promise."

He tapped her hand. She spent most of the morning with her parents. Russ mowed the lawn while she baked some cookies with Sheila. Her mother liked delivering a fresh batch of cookies to the day care, which opened on a Saturday. While they were talking, her mother opened up about her father's indiscretions and also admitted that she'd forced him out of their life after the loss of her unborn baby. The miscarriage had hit her mother hard, hard enough to hate her father. Once he came home after cheating on her with another woman, he'd sobbed out all of his loss and the love he had for Sheila. Holly was happy that her mother opened up to her about it.

When her mother left to deliver the cookies she asked her father for a ride to the clubhouse. She wanted to see Duke before she headed home or at least went to his home.

Holly climbed off the back of his bike, kissing his cheek.

Several guys were outside. One of them was Daisy.

"Hey," she said. "Duke in there?"

"He sure is."

Entering the clubhouse she was aware of gazes on her. Her heart raced at the thought of what they were all thinking. She didn't stop to give any of them any notice. The door closed behind her, and she saw Mandy was serving at the main bar. Some of the guys were drinking. Most of the men were in mechanics' overalls covered with grease stains. She heard Duke before she saw him. He held a pool stick and had just taken his shot.

Linda hung off Knuckles as they were playing pool together. Duke didn't have anyone hanging off him, which she liked.

Drawing her shoulders back, she advanced toward her man. He'd not noticed her yet.

Duke turned toward her when she was only a few steps away. He didn't say anything, merely watched her.

"Hey," she said, moving in front of him.

"Hey."

One of his brows rose, waiting for her. It was all on her what she decided to do. Running her hands up his chest, she banded them around his neck, drawing his head down for a kiss. The club faded away for her. Duke dropped the pool stick. She heard it fall to the floor with a clatter. He gripped her hips lifting her onto the pool table.

Holly moaned, kissing him back with an equal passion. Her pussy grew slick, and her nipples went rock hard. She needed him.

"Fuck, baby," he said, breaking away from the kiss.

"No more hiding. No more secrets." She slid her hands down to grip his ass, pulling him closer.

He didn't give her a chance to say anything more. Duke lifted her up in his arms and took her toward church.

Catcalls and whistles followed after them. They were shut out when he kicked the door closed.

Duke put her on her feet. "Take your clothes off."

Chapter Ten

Duke went to his belt as he watched Holly wriggle out of her jeans. She hadn't changed the clothes she'd put on that morning, and wasn't wearing any panties. Her bare pussy was slick.

"Climb onto the table." He needed inside her more than he needed his next breath. Duke had seen her enter the club, but he'd waited. He'd promised her that she could decide when they no longer were a secret. Russ already called him to let him know she'd visited him. The loyalty shown by his club touched him even though Holly hadn't kept him in the dark. She'd texted him each step of the way.

Holly used the chair to ease her onto the table.

"Everyone knows who you belong to."

She nodded, going to her elbows. He stepped closer, lifting her legs to rest on the arms of both chairs. Her chest rose and fell with each indrawn breath she took. "You want my dick in that sweet little pussy?" he asked, pulling his cock out.

"Yes."

"Then play with your pussy. Let me see how wet you are." Her fingers reached down going on either side of her plump lips. She made his mouth water for a taste of her. Duke worked his length as he watched her finger move over her clit. "Don't orgasm. You orgasm before I tell you then you don't get my cock."

She released a whimper, but he ignored it. He was the man in charge, not her.

Down she moved her fingers until she circled the entrance of her cunt. "Hold your lips open," he said.

Both of her hands eased down, opening her slit for him. He saw her entrance ease open. She was soaking wet. Gripping the tip of his cock, he placed it where she needed him most.

"Don't move your hands. You keep your pussy open for me."

She nodded.

Sliding inside her, Duke groaned at the tightness of her. No matter how much he fucked her she always felt unbearably tight. His balls tightened, and he wrapped his fingers around her knees.

He caressed down her legs until he gripped her hips. Holly gasped as he drew her onto his cock. Her fingers stayed between them, keeping her open for his cock.

In one slam of his hips, he seated himself to the hilt inside her. He waited, allowing her to get accustomed to his length.

"Fuck, baby, you've got no idea how fucking hot you look, taking my cock. Look at us. Watch as I fuck you."

He eased out of her. His length covered in her slick cream. Duke watched as she stared at where they were connected.

Tightening his hands on her already bruised hips, he fucked hard inside her. She screamed out. He didn't care if the brothers heard him. They all knew he'd be fucking her inside this room. It would only be a matter of time before he took her as his old lady.

"Now, you can play with your pretty pussy."

Her fingers moved to her clit.

"Let me lick you."

She presented her other fingers to his lips. He sucked her cream from her fingers, relishing the taste of her.

The sounds of their flesh slapping together filled the room.

"Come for me, Holly. Come all over my cock."

Staring down at where they were joined he watched her fingers work her clit. Her pussy tightened around his shaft, and within seconds she splintered apart.

Slamming inside her, Duke closed his eyes, yelling as he came within her depths. Collapsing over her, he pressed kisses to each of her breasts, sucking the buds into his mouth. The pleasure didn't immediately ebb away. She ran her fingers through his hair. The only sound in the room was their heavy breathing.

"Everyone would have heard us fucking, wouldn't they?" she asked.

"Yeah."

"Can I ask you something?"

He looked up. "Yes."

"When I was at my parents' place—"

Duke groaned. "You want to talk about your parents with my dick inside you."

"When I was at my parents', I mentioned about you taking me as your old lady. I hate the term, but I know it's what you use to make the difference between a club whore and an old lady."

"What about it?" he asked.

"They shared a look. My mom looked worried. Why?"

He let out a breath. He wasn't going to tell her about what becoming an old lady meant. Not after he'd just fucked her with the men in the other room. She'd run. There would be a time in a couple of weeks when he'd tell her truth. "It's a huge commitment, Holly. It's not something to be taken lightly."

"I wouldn't take it lightly."

"Some might." He pressed a kiss to her lips.

"You're not telling me everything."

He let out a sigh. "I'll tell you more about it soon. I promise. You're not ready to know." He eased out of her ordering her to stay still.

Duke grabbed some tissues and wiped his seed from her bare lips.

The sight of his white cum leaking out of her cunt had him getting thicker once again. The sight was fucking hot. He held the tissue in one hand, and with the other, he ran his fingers through her red, swollen flesh, pushing his seed back inside her. In a couple of years he'd have her pregnant with his kid. She'd make one hell of a mother.

She gasped, shaking as he worked his cum inside her.

Wiping his fingers on the tissue, he grabbed her jeans, and helped her to dress.

"Julie came by earlier," he said, buttoning up her jeans.

"Why?" she asked. There was no jealousy to her voice. She looked annoyed more than anything.

"She started shouting shit out about you."

"She knew about me?"

He nodded. "I don't know how she knew, but she did. I'm going to find out how, but until I do, Daisy and several brothers are going to be taking care of you."

"Tailing me?"

"Yeah, don't argue. If Julie comes near you and they can't intervene, I want you to walk away. Call me, do whatever you need to do, but do not talk to her."

"I won't."

He wrapped his arms around her body, gripping her plump ass. "Are you coming back to my place?"

"I will. I want to talk to Pike first."

Groaning, he shook his head. "We've got to leave Mary and Pike to their own problems."

"She's my friend."

"So is Pike," Duke said.

"He fucked her last night."

"Holly, baby, I fucked you last night. You've got to leave them alone. Their shit is their own."

He tilted her head back, forcing her to look at him.

"I worry about her."

"I'm not going to get between my boys' relationships. Mary knows what she's getting herself into. She's not naive about the club."

"You're right. She did tell me to leave it alone."

"Then leave it alone. Come on, I better take over from Raoul." He took her hand, heading out of the clubhouse.

Several brothers nodded their head toward him. They glanced at Holly, but none of them said a word. Russ had already had a word with all the men. They knew shit was serious between him and Holly. He wasn't using her for some quick fun. It was the real deal for him.

When they got to his bike, he glanced at her.

"Maybe I should call you a cab," he said.

She shook her head. "You've got to be crazy. I'm not some newbie here, Duke. I've been on the back of my dad's bike plenty. Who do you think brought me here?"

"Your dad did? On the back of his bike?"

She nodded her head to both questions.

"I'm not some kind of bike virgin. I know how to hold on at your back."

Duke grabbed a helmet and handed it to her. "You're not getting on the back of my bike without a helmet."

She rolled her eyes but put one on. "How do I look?"

"Hot."

Holly rolled her eyes once again.

"You keep that up and you're going to be going over my knee."

"Do you promise?" she asked.

He liked this side to his woman. It had been too damn long since he had such fun.

"Get on the back of my bike before I take you right here." He straddled his bike, and she climbed on behind him. Duke would have to tell her about the club's rule. When he'd been married to Julie, they'd argued repeatedly about him taking her like the other old ladies. He never would.

Taking an old lady was about respect, showing the brothers a part of yourself you never left exposed.

She held on tight, and he pulled out of the clubhouse. In all the years he'd been with Julie he'd never once felt anything close for her. Holly, they'd been together a matter of weeks and he knew this was it for him. There wouldn't be another woman in his life.

****

The next couple of weeks were a whirlwind of pleasure throughout. She spent most of her time at Duke's place, and when she wasn't working at the nursery, she was with him. He didn't give her a chance to be alone, calling her the moment she got off work. She did get the chance to spend a little time with Mary over the last couple of weeks, not enough though. Mary started dating Mac from the diner. Nothing had happened yet but Holly didn't like it.

She walked out of the nursery at three Wednesday afternoon about to text Duke when someone stepped in front of her.

Glancing at the person in front of her, she found Julie glaring at her. "It's about time we had a little talk."

Julie was pale, sweating, and looking withdrawn. Duke had warned her about Julie's use of narcotics. Holly quickly sent him a text letting him know Julie was waiting for her. Mothers were leaving with their children, but a couple stopped to watch them. Holly hated the attention. She should have known it would only be a matter of time before Julie stopped by to see her.

"What do you want, Julie?" she asked, pulling her bag high onto her shoulder.

"You think you're fucking smart spreading your legs for Duke. You're nothing but a whore in a long line of filthy bitches."

Holly hated being called names or being sneered at. The disgust on Julie's face was evident. Her cell phone buzzed, and she looked down at the screen.

Duke: On way!

Until he arrived she was alone.

"Look, I don't know what your problem is. I'm dating Duke—"

"You've always wanted Duke. How do I know you've not fucked him before now? Tempting him with that young fucking pussy of yours."

Heat filled Holly's cheeks at her words. She didn't want her private life coming to light.

"Never. Duke wouldn't have done that to you. I was underage. Don't ever insinuate shit like that." She took a step closer to Julie.

"Your age doesn't bother him now."

Gritting her teeth, Holly shook her head. "This is why you're never going to get back with him. You're an embarrassment. When was the last time you even called Matthew?" She hadn't. Matthew didn't care much, but there had to be a small spark of pain. This woman, this bitch, was his mother. It had to hurt to know she didn't care about him.

"Don't even try to bring that boy into this."

"Do you even know his fucking name?"

Before Holly could react, Julie brought her hand across her face. Holly hadn't expected the slap. She stumbled back.

"Duke's mine. You're just a young fucking whore who doesn't know how to keep her legs fucking closed."

Stepping forward, Holly stood her ground. If it wasn't for the children around them, she'd have Julie on the floor. She wouldn't do anything to upset the kids.

"Try that again."

Julie raised her fist. Before she got a chance to do anything, Duke pulled her back. "I suggest you get out of here and heed my warning before I make sure the only air you'll be breathing will be filled with the scent and taste of dirt." Duke pushed Julie toward a waiting Pike. "Get her out of here, now."

Duke moved toward Holly. "Are you okay?"

"I'm fine. I was expecting her to come for me." She pressed her palm to her stinging cheek. "Your ex is a physcho."

He chuckled. "Come on, let's get you home."

She followed him to his bike, climbing on behind him. Resting her stinging cheek against the leather of his cut, she breathed him in. The machine gunned out of the town. He passed the apartment and took her straight to his ranch.

Once they were inside he settled her down on a chair at the counter. "Why didn't you hit her back?" Duke asked, pressing a bag of frozen peas against her cheek.

"Kids were there watching. I didn't want to create a scene by lashing out." She stared up at him. His arms were folded across his chest. "Next time I'll hit her. For a skinny woman, she's got a lot of muscle behind her." Her cheek was stinging.

"Julie's a law unto herself. I don't know what to do with her."

"What do you mean?" she asked, dropping the peas when the cold got too much for her.

"She's hanging out with some bad guys." He mentioned a crew she hadn't heard of. "I want you to be careful. Julie has always been unstable." He stroked the backs of his fingers down her cheek, the anger clear on his face. "If she'd been anyone else."

"Being Matthew's mother gives her a lot of leeway. You don't need to do anything about her, Duke. It was a slap. She said some pretty hurtful things as well. I think she's still in love with you."

"What shit did she say?"

Holly told him, to which he cursed. "I wouldn't have touched you underage even if you begged me, Holly."

"I know that. It wasn't even on my mind. She's messing with us, and I don't want her to do that." She placed the peas on the counter, standing up so he wasn't towering over her so much. It didn't help. Duke towered over her regardless.

"There's something else I've got to tell you. It's about becoming my old lady."

He'd put off telling her the last couple of weeks. Matthew was out with friends as school was out for the summer. The nursery still ran, but it was more a daycare center to help the local families.

"What?"

Duke looked torn. "I don't want anyone else to tell you the truth."

"Okay, you're starting to freak me out a little. It can't be that bad." She touched his hand, linking their fingers together.

He touched her cheek. "Each club has their own rules for bringing in club whores and old ladies. For a club whore, she is displayed in front of the club and men use her."

"Use her?"

"Fuck her. It can be any way providing she brings men to orgasm."

She was going to be sick. "Oh God."

"It's safe and consensual, Holly. Every woman who does it knows her place within the club."

"What about an old lady?" She thought about her mother. The look Sheila and her father shared. Was this the reason?

"For an old lady, it's different but not by much."

"What?" Holly didn't know what to make of what he was saying.

He held her hands tightly, refusing to let her go. "The club needs to know your place within the club. An old lady is different than a club whore, but she is taken in front of the club."

"Taken?"

"Fucked."

Her stomach turned over. "By other men?" The thought of another man touching her left her sick to her stomach.

"No. An old lady is cherished. Only the man she's agreed to marry, to share her life with, is with her."

"You're telling me you want to fuck me in a room full of men I've known my whole life, for what?"

"They'll know you're loyal to the club, to me, and in return you'll get their protection."

"Why can't you just put a ring on my finger?"

"Each club is different. This is one of the rules that the guys agreed to. By taking you in front of them, it's showing to them you're special to me."

"But so are the club whores."

"Not in the same way."

Tears filled her eyes, and she took a step away from him. He didn't let her go. Duke held her hands.

"Did you do this for Julie?"

"No, and she didn't get the protection along with it. Your mother, she's protected by the club."

"My dad?"

"He won't be there, but of course he knows what it is."

"I don't know if I can do that."

"I can wait. It's for your protection as much as anything."

"To let men get off or mock me for being with you?"

"They wouldn't dare to mock you."

Tears filled her eyes. Duke was different from all of the other men. There was no way she was ever going to be naked with the club looking on, Raoul mocking her. "I need to go home." She tugged on her hand, trying to get him to leave her alone.

"I'm not letting you go like this."

"I need to think about this."

"Holly, stay."

"Duke, let me go."

He tugged her close, banding his arm around her waist. "Know this, Holly. You will be my woman and my old lady. You're not getting away from me. I won't let you. I love you, and I know you love me."

"This is awful."

"Think about your mother, Holly. Did she ever get treated with anything but respect?"

She shook her head, biting her lip at the same time.

"You'll never be mocked, and no one will ever bring it up. It's the secrecy of the club, the loyalty. You may go back home, but you don't get to tell Mary about this."

"She's my friend."

"She's not club. No one must know."

Holly nodded. "Then can I make a phone call? I want to talk to my mom."

"Yes." He dropped a kiss to her lips. "I'm going to be back at the clubhouse. I've got some business to deal with."

He'd already done a run a few weeks back. It was the only time they'd been apart. She'd stayed here to be with Matthew while Duke was out of town.

"I'll be back."

"I won't leave."

Duke kissed her one final time before heading out of the house. Grabbing her cell phone from her pocket, she dialed her mother.

"Hey, honey, it has been a long time since you called me."

Holly let the tears fall down her cheeks as she stared down at the ground. What should she say to her mom?

"Holly?"

"I'm here." Her voice sounded croaky even to her.

"What's the matter, honey? What's happened?"

"Duke, he told me about the old lady thing. Is it true?"

She got her answer when her mother was silent on the other end.

"You fucked Dad with other men watching?" Holly asked, accusingly.

"Holly Crock, I do not care how old you are. Do not even think to use that tone with me."

"I don't understand."

"You'll never understand how important it is until you do it. I can't talk to you about what happened. It's the rules of the club. What I can say to you is you don't have to be afraid. The club will show you respect. I've never been embarrassed, and I will not be now."

Holly broke down listening to her mother talk. She didn't know if she was strong enough to be everything Duke wanted her to be.

"Do you love him?" Sheila asked, minutes later.

"What?"

"Duke, do you love him? Is he all you think about?"

"Yes."

"Then trust me when I say you can do this. It's important to your man and to the club. He wouldn't do it for Julie, but he's doing this for you."

Several minutes later Holly said goodbye to her mother and hung up the phone. Glancing over at the clock she saw it had been well over an hour since Duke had left.

Chapter Eleven

Duke walked in home to find Holly and Matthew playing a game of cards. Every time he saw her with his son it was like he was kicked in the gut in a good way. Julie wouldn't have taken the time to play with him, yet Holly, she always laughed, including his son. The scent of chicken and garlic permeated the air. Part of him had expected her to be gone after their conversation. Sheila called him at the clubhouse while he was dealing with Diaz. She'd done her best to help her daughter to understand, but the rest of it was up to him.

He removed his cut hanging it along with the other jackets before going further into his house.

"Hey, Dad," Matthew said. "I'm getting my ass kicked by a girl."

Holly burst out laughing.

"Don't worry about it, son. She's trained with the best and will always be the best." He had no doubt that Russ trained her well. Going past his woman, he leaned down to kiss her neck. "I'm grabbing a beer."

"Sure, Dad."

Holly didn't say anything. He'd noticed she didn't tense up either from his touch. Entering the kitchen, he went straight for the fridge, grabbing a beer.

"Hey," she said.

Duke turned to find Holly leaning against the counter with her arms crossed beneath her breasts.

"You talked with your mother?"

"Yes."

He gave her his full attention. Popping the lid off the beer, he took a long swallow. With her being in his place was she going to stay? Even if she left he'd have given her tonight to work her shit out before going back for her.

She needed to realize they were a done deal. It wouldn't matter what went on in their personal lives, they were a couple.

"Here, I got you this," he said, pulling out the ring he got her. He couldn't ride his bike with the ring in the box so he'd pushed it into his jeans pocket, discarding the box.

Holly took a step toward him. He placed the diamond ring in her hand and simply watched her.

"What is this?" she asked.

"An engagement ring." A damn expensive one, too.

"You're proposing to me?"

"Isn't that what it looks like?" He'd never really proposed to anyone. When Julie told him she was pregnant, he took a quick trip to Vegas and they were married by the weekend.

"No. This is the strangest proposal of all."

He reached out to stroke her cheek. "I love you, Holly. I'm going to spend the rest of my life showing you how much I love you. I don't give a fuck how old I am. I'm going to show you the world, and I want us to do it together."

Tears filled her eyes, and he wiped them away as they spilled down her cheeks.

"I love you, Duke."

"If you don't want to be my old lady, fine, but at least be my wife."

"You're willing to not, erm, take me in front of the club?" she asked, biting her lip.

"Baby, the only woman I've ever loved is standing right in front of me. You don't want me to take you in front of the club, be my old lady, fine. I'll take you as my wife." Duke leaned down, brushing his lips across hers. He'd always worry about her safety, but he'd take whatever he could get.

"I want to be your old lady, Duke."

He leaned back to look into her eyes. She offered him a watery smile. "Are you sure?" he asked.

"I'm sure. I love you. I'm just worried about what the others will think." She shrugged. "So long as I'm with you, I really don't care. You're the man I want to be with. No one else."

Wrapping his arms around her, Duke pulled her close. "I'll get everything set up."

She nodded. She gripped his arms tighter, and he felt the hard bite of her nails against his flesh.

He kissed the top of her head, inhaling her scent.

"My parents won't be present?"

"No, of course not." He chuckled, pulling away.

"Good. I won't be able to go through with it."

Duke tucked some hair behind her ears, smiling down at her. "Feed me, woman."

She slapped his arm, moving around him to grab dinner out of the oven.

Going into the dining room he saw Matthew setting the table. "Have you made a decision about your mom?" Duke asked.

He was waiting for Matthew to decide if he still wanted to spend any time with Julie in the future. Duke didn't yet have any plans to kill the woman, but if she kept causing problems then he wouldn't hesitate.

The news from Dawg's Crew was not good. From what he'd been told Julie was selling her pussy for free drugs. It would only be a matter of time before that shit started to go nasty. He wouldn't be able to let it continue. Duke's ex selling pussy was not a rumor he wanted going around. It made him look weak. If he looked weak, so did his MC. He wouldn't allow that.

"Dad, I don't know. I don't like her, okay. I don't even want to be near her. She's always saying shit about you, but she's still my mom."

"Is that what Holly's said?" Duke asked.

"Yeah, maybe I should give her a chance to be a real mom. I mean, if she's going to keep trying to do the right thing, maybe I should give her a chance."

"She's your mother. I love you, son. If you want her to remain in your life then that's your call."

"Then, for now, she stays. Can I stay here though?"

"This is your house."

Holly walked in carrying a tray full with chicken. His woman knew exactly what to serve him. He always loved a woman who knew how to cook. The rest of the evening went by without a hitch. They ate as a family and watched a movie after he and Matthew did the dishes. Holly wore the ring he gave her. He stroked his thumb over the ring. It was his claim to Holly, and no other man was going to take her away.

****

Days passed, and Holly didn't know what to think as Duke hadn't told her about the old lady thing. That was how she referred to it in her mind, "old lady thing". Every chance she got she showed the ring off to anyone who wanted to see. It was a beautiful diamond ring, simple yet stunning. She loved it and found herself staring at it. For years she had wanted to get to know Duke. It almost seemed too surreal for her to be sleeping beside him, loving him, fucking him.

Sitting in the diner she waited for Mary to have a break. She didn't like the relationship budding between her friend and Mac. The owner of the diner seemed to always have an agenda.

Sipping her coffee, she watched Mary move from table to table as Mac rang out the orders. The diner was a popular place to eat. With Mary in charge of the food, it would soon make its stamp on the map as a place to visit. Was that Mac's agenda? Get Mary in the kitchen cooking? Mac was a good cook but nothing compared to Mary's awesomeness. Even Holly couldn't compete with Mary's natural way in the kitchen.

Her cell phone buzzed pulling her out of her troubled thoughts.

Duke: Hey, baby, how ya doin?

Holly: I'm at the diner. Don't like Mac's attention on my girl. Guy gives me the creeps.

He didn't. Mac was just a guy who used everything at his disposal.

Duke: u've got 2 stop worrying so much. Mary's a big girl. She can take care of herself.

Holly: She's my friend. Y u texting?

There were a few seconds before he responded.

Duke: Come 2 the club 2night.

She gripped the phone tighter.

"Hey, sorry I took so long. It's a busy lunch today. Sharon's taking over." Mary squeezed into the booth opposite her, and she poured herself a coffee.

Duke: Holly?

"Don't worry about it. Are we going to order, or are you really busy?"

Holly: Fine.

Rubbing her head, she stared across at Mary.

"Let's eat. It has been too long since we caught up."

Nodding, she glanced over the menu as the doorbell rang. Looking up she saw Pike, Raoul, and a couple of the club whores entered the diner. Mary checked the door at the same time. The moment her friend tensed, Holly knew she'd seen them.

"We can go elsewhere if you want?" Holly said.

"No. I want to stay here. Nothing is going to happen." Mary smiled up at her.

Holly stayed silent as Pike stopped by the table. "Hello, ladies."

"Hey," Holly said.

"Hey." Mary didn't look up from her menu, giving Pike the brush off.

"Can we sit with you?" Pike asked.

"No." Before Holly got a chance to speak, Mary took control.

"Why not?" Pike folded his arms over his chest. The woman behind him chose that moment to wrap her arms around his waist.

If she didn't know Mary as well as she did, she wouldn't have seen the hurt flash in her eyes. Holly knew her friend well. Mary was hurting.

"I'm not part of the club. You're all part of the club."

"Holly's part of the club," Pike said.

"She's spending lunch with me. I'm not club, so I don't count. There are plenty of tables for you and your club." Mary went back to looking over her menu.

"Are you going to let her talk to you like that?" Mandy asked. Holly recognized her from the club. She remembered what Duke said about the whores earning their place. Had Duke helped to bring Mandy into the club?

Don't think about that. It's all in the past.

Pike stared at Mary while she did everything to not look at him.

Seconds that felt like minutes passed before Pike turned away. "Come on, we can have another table."

Mary continued to look over the menu.

"I know you care about him."

"My feelings about him do not matter. He told me that. I'm not club. I'll never be part of the club. I was just a one-night stand to him."

Holly's temper flared. "Did that bastard say that to you?"

"No, he didn't need to say it. I know what I mean to him or what I don't mean to him."

"I'll kick his ass."

"No, you won't. What happened between me and Pike is none of your business. I love you, Hols, I really do. Please, forget about him. I intend to."

She wanted to argue but saw Mary was determined to let it go. Relaxing down into her seat, Holly tried to forget about Duke's text message. He wanted her to come to the club tonight. Did that mean what she thought it would mean? God, she was so confused. Her emotions were all over the place.

Running fingers through her hair, she decided to put all of her worries to the back of her mind and simply focus on her friend. Mary needed her right now.

They ate burgers together, drank coffee, and just talked. They were organizing her wedding with Mary. Her mother, Sheila, was also helping to plan the event.

Holly hoped to have a Christmas wedding, but it would depend on what Duke wanted. Everything was moving so fast, yet far from being terrified, she was excited.

Chapter Twelve

"You better take care of my baby," Russ said, pointing a finger at Duke.

"I will, sir, I promise."

"Okay, Sheila's already made plans for us tonight." Russ tapped him on the shoulder. "You did a good run. A good investment."

Duke had shared the three million among all members of the club. They'd each taken their cash to be stored until they could use it safely. The money could be spent on small things, grocery shopping, a few minor debts that were in the hundreds, but nothing in the thousands as that brought attention.

"Ned's happy with the deal."

"The Skulls are taking a break," Russ said. "I can't blame them. They're a good crew and have been through a lot of shit. When's the next ride?"

"Not for a couple of months." This was what Duke liked about dealing with Ned and Diaz. The work was regular but not dangerously close together. They were just starting out, so every few months they'd have a big shipment. Once they proved their worth, more jobs would come their way. In the meantime, Duke could get his house finished, and get the mechanics shop back up to being the best in town. They were only repairing a couple of cars a week. Duke knew they could be doing a few cars a day.

"Right, I'm out of here." Russ slapped him on the back. "Treat her right."

He watched Russ walk out of the club without a backward glance. Duke didn't need to respond to Russ. He had every intention of treating his woman, right.

Declining a beer, he stood up, and headed toward church. He stopped when he found Raoul sitting at the table, staring at the insignia inscribed into it.

"What are you doing in here?"

"I never meant to say the shit I did. I didn't even want it to go as far as it did that night," Raoul said, glancing up at Duke. "I know you sent me to be with Holly because I was closer to her age. I don't know what the fuck happened that night. We were dancing, having a lot of fun. I've always liked Holly, and that night I finally saw what you did."

Duke glared at the men. Neither of them had spoken about his involvement with Raoul taking Holly to the prom.

"She was beautiful, fun, alive, happy. When we got the room and she asked me to make love to her, I did. I didn't even think about the consequences. When it was over, I knew I'd screwed up." Raoul glanced up at Duke. "I fucked up, and you'll never understand how sorry I am for what I did."

"Where's this going?" Duke asked, folding his arms.

"Phil, he's the eyes for Dawg's team. I did some digging, and the bastard has a serious gambling problem. He owes Dawg a shitload of money. Telling him about your whereabouts, including Holly's, is what he had to do to pay them back. I don't know if the debt is covered." Raoul pulled out a folded piece of paper. "I know you want me out of the club, but I'm going to prove to you that I'm worth keeping around. I respect Holly. She's a good woman and part of the reason I shot my mouth off was because of that."

"That makes no fucking sense," Duke said, snatching the paper out of Raoul's grip.

"I treated her like shit. She didn't give me a thought. You wanted her, and I didn't want to come between you." Raoul took a step toward the door.

"Wait." Duke glanced down at the paperwork in his hands. He turned toward Raoul. "Thank you."

"I like Holly. I'll never treat her like shit again. I promise." Raoul offered his hand to which Duke shook. "The club will always come first."

He watched Raoul leave church. When he was alone he took a seat and glanced over the figures that he'd been given. There was no way some information would cover this amount of debt. Pulling out his cell phone he dialed the Sheriff.

"Hey, David, I've got some information here that doesn't look too good for your deputy."

When Duke was finished on the phone, he heard a faint knock on the door.

"Come in."

David was going to have a word with Phil, and his place as a deputy was now out of the picture. Duke didn't care. The bastard was willing to tell club secrets, he answered for his actions.

"Hey," Holly said, drawing his attention toward her.

His cock thickened at the sight of her. She wore a long denim skirt with a white blouse. His woman looked good enough to eat, let alone fuck.

Getting to his feet, he pulled her against him. "Hello, baby." He drew her close, gripping her ass as he claimed a kiss. "I missed you."

"I missed you, too."

He rubbed his nose against hers, smiling. There was nothing he wouldn't do to protect this woman. She controlled him in ways she didn't even begin to understand, and he knew he held the same control over her.

Her hand shook when he locked their fingers together. "Are you nervous?"

"Wouldn't you be?"

"The only thing I've been nervous about is telling you the truth of how we take old ladies."

Duke watched as she tucked some hair behind her ear. "I'd be lying if I said I wasn't nervous. I'm nervous, but I want to be with you. I love you, Duke."

"You've got nothing to be nervous about. Come on, let's go and enjoy the others' company."

He led her out of church, leading her toward the bar. It was past six, yet it was still light out. In a few weeks that would all be changing as fall started to take effect. He loved the fall, loved Christmas at the ranch. When the house was covered in snow, the lawns white, it was a beautiful sight to witness. This year he'd be spending it with Holly.

Sheila had told him about Holly's wish for them to be married at Christmas. He'd give her the proper wedding she deserved. There would be no expense spared for his woman.

Duke sat her at the bar, ordering them both a beer.

"A little courage. Enjoy it," he said. "This is your first and last one of the night."

She laughed, taking small sips. The club was in full party mode. This was what he loved about his club. After a long ride, the chance to kick back and relax was always the best. It had been a couple of weeks since the ride, but this was the first chance they'd gotten to actually kick back. Club business never stopped. Being a father also never stopped.

Matthew was spending the night with his mother, at his own request, which sure as fuck surprised Duke. He hoped Julie didn't fuck it up. Their son was pretty special.

Mandy and Pike were playing pool at the only table. The couple was all over each other.

"Do you want to play?" Duke asked.

"Are you good?"

"Yeah."

"If we win, can you get Pike to tell me the truth about him and Mary?"

"Not tonight but another night I will make him and he'll tell me," he said, answering honestly.

"Do you promise to tell me what he says?" she asked.

"Yeah."

"Then let's play."

Holly took another swig from her bottle as they made their way toward the club. Duke wouldn't take her right away. The party needed to calm down first.

"Want to play?" Duke asked, raising a brow at Pike.

"Sure."

"What we're playing for?" Mandy asked.

"Truth," Holly said, glaring at the club whore.

"Truth?" Pike kept his gaze on him.

"Yeah."

"Do I get to know what this truth is about?" Pike asked.

Duke pulled his woman closer to him, covering her mouth as he spoke. "Not until we play."

"Okay, so you want a truth if you win. What do I get?" Pike asked.

"I'll do your laundry for a week and cook for you," Holly said.

"Deal." There was no hesitation in Pike. Duke didn't doubt the man that he knew what the truth was about.

"Who gets to shoot first?" Pike asked.

Duke glanced at Holly, who shrugged back at him. "You chose."

"Okay, I'll shoot first."

The game had finally started.

****

Duke won the game with the promise of getting the truth out of Pike. The rest of the night Holly stayed by Duke's side. They either danced to the loud music, played pool, or cards. The party was amazing. She loved every second of it. The guys were all being nice to her, accepting her into their fold. She felt their acceptance of her. Their gazes locked on her and Duke throughout the night, waiting, the anticipation driving the need inside her.

This was what it meant to be part of the club. It was only a matter of time before Duke took it to the next level. She wasn't stupid. He was biding his time for the right moment.

Duke was priming her for the occasion. He took every opportunity he could find to kiss or touch her. She loved his touch. The way he stroked his fingers up the inside of her thighs had her melting against him. He easily lifted up the denim skirt to find her skin beneath.

The hours passed, the drinking toned down, and the music became slow, sensual. Holly felt the answering call inside her. When he'd first told her about sex in front of the club, she'd been disgusted, but now she just wanted him with a passion that surprised her. She stood in Duke's arms as they danced to the music. Closing her eyes, she was almost hypnotized by the pleasure of it all. Her pussy was slick to the touch. Duke gripped her ass, making her very aware of the state of his arousal. Each second that past only heightened her arousal further. She wanted him badly. It no longer mattered to her that the club was about to see her getting fucked. The only thing on her mind was Duke.

He tilted her head back with a finger underneath her chin. The rest of the room fell away as he looked at her with his dark brown eyes. His head drew nearer, and a second later, his lips were on hers. She opened her mouth, accepting his kiss, his touch, his love.

The hand on her chin moved up to sink inside her hair.

She moaned, wrapping her arms around his neck. The music continued to play as Duke deepened the kiss.

His tongue met with hers, creating a dance inside her mouth. Duke moved her back until she pressed against a post that faced the whole of the room. She kept her eyes closed as he kissed down her neck. For a split second she just had to know what was going on, so she opened her eyes. The men were sat in their places, giving them enough distance. There was no disgust on their faces. She saw their respect as Duke kissed and sucked on her neck. They were not here to judge her. They were here to accept her not as Russ's kid but as Duke's woman. Each of their gazes was on them, none of them looking away.

Staring at Duke, she pushed all of her negativity aside and focused on him.

The room fell away. She forgot about the men and women about to witness her become part of Duke.

"Think about me, Holly. Only me." He whispered the words beside her ear.

Running her hands underneath his jacket, he caught her wrists together placing them above her head.

"I'm the one in control here."

She nodded, finally opening her eyes to stare back at him. The lust was clear to see in his gaze.

"Fuck me, Duke." Holly gaze herself to him. He picked her up and carried her over to the pool table, which the men had stopped playing. The angle of the table meant they could still see them together but offered them some semblance of privacy.

He lifted up her skirt until it pooled around her waist. She wanted him so damn bad.

"Look at them, Holly. Look into their eyes. They don't hate you or find disgust here. They respect you for taking me, for loving me, for being loyal to the club. You're offering yourself to me, trusting me."

She glanced over to the men, expecting to see something else in their gaze than she'd seen moments ago. Their respect was still there, but now she saw something else. What she saw was heated lust in all of their gazes. This was what the old ladies went through to be part of the club. They were promising to take care of her along with any children she might have. All she needed to do was promise herself to Duke and the club.

"Fuck, baby, you're so wet for me." He ran his fingers through her slit, making her ache with need for him.

"Please, Duke."

He teased her clit, sliding down to fuck into her pussy. "Remove your shirt and take your bra off."

Pulling her shirt over her head, she cried out as he fucked two fingers inside her as he stroked her with his thumb. She was thrust into pleasure as he worked her body. Closing her eyes, she gave herself to him, letting Duke take control. There was no fight inside her.

She loved the man who was now giving her pleasure that she didn't think was possible to feel. This was what it meant to be part of his life, to be in the club. She'd do it because she loved Duke.

"Come for me, Holly." He flicked her clit, drawing a cry from her lips. She glanced down to see his hand between her thighs. "Lie back."

Lying back, she moaned as he withdrew his hand, leaving her empty of his touch. Holly started to beg him for his hands on her.

Duke didn't give her anything. The only touch she got was the touch he wanted her to have. Biting her lip, she whimpered.

The tip of his cock replaced his fingers. "I love you, Holly. I chose you as my old lady."

He slid inside her, inch after inch. Gripping his hands, she gasped as he played with her clit with each plunge of his hips. He was riding her pussy as he pulled her closer to orgasm.

"So beautiful, all mine."

Holly screamed as with one slam he embedded himself deep inside her. He was so long and thick that it was on the verge of pain. She didn't care, giving herself to him as fucked her hard throughout her orgasm. In the background she heard several masculine moans, and when she turned her head, she saw they were touching themselves. No other cock was visible, but their hands were rubbing themselves through their pants.

He tugged her up so that she was on the end of the pool table with his cock still deep inside her.

Duke slammed his lips down on hers, burning her alive with the possession of his cock and the touch of his lips. He drove her to the peak of bliss once again but wouldn't let her go over the edge. Duke wore his jacket as he made his claim.

"I love you," he said.

"I love you, too."

"Come for me." His one instruction and she went up in flames in his arms, screaming his name. She held onto him throughout the pleasure that tilted her world. He tightened his arms around her and growled as his cock jerked, filling her with his cum. When it was over, she looked up as he removed his jacket, placing the leather cut over her body. "Mine, all mine."

She smiled up at him, touching his face.

He glanced over her shoulder, and she looked behind her to see the intensity in the men's gazes. They were still locked on them.

"I expect you to treat her with care and respect. She's club now. You will never turn your back on her."

They all stood up putting their hands to their chests.

"Trojans forever."

Each member chanted the words, "Trojans forever". The fervor inside them infected her with it. This was what the club was. They took care of their own.

"Come on, I'm taking you up to my room," Duke said, lifting her up in his arms.

She held onto him as he made his way toward the back stairs. Some men lived in the clubhouse completely while others went home at night. Duke carried her up three flights of stairs until they came to the top bedroom.

He placed her on her feet, turning her to look at him.

"Thank you," she said, pressing her palm over his heart. "You made that easy for me."

"I know you, Holly. I'll always do what you need, but remember, I'm the one in control here."

Holly smiled up at him. "I know."

"Don't ever think you can tame shit down when we're in the privacy of our own bedroom. I want the wildcat you've shown me you can be."

Keeping his jacket on, she dropped the skirt and panties until she stood before him in only his jacket. "Like this?" she asked, giving him a twirl of her naked in front of him.

"Fuck, baby, you're so fucking beautiful." He carried her to the bed, showing her exactly what he wanted in the privacy of his own bedroom. She had no doubt who was in control, and she loved every second of it.

Chapter Thirteen

Three weeks later

Holly helped to carry the cakes toward the diner with Mary. There was a competition going on in the diner that Mac had organized. They had two entries, one of them Mary's, the other Holly's. The winner got to have their cake added to the menu.

She'd settled on a traditional carrot cake while Mary baked a double chocolate, fudgy cake. There was going to be no doubt of the winner, but it was offering to be a little fun. The Trojans were going to be present for the tasting within the diner, which was proving to be a big hit. They entered the diner to see something in the range of fifty cakes.

"Here, Holly," Mary said, pointing at two clear places for them to put their cakes.

"This is an amazing turnout." Holly wore one of Duke's leather jackets, showing her claim as his old lady. No one messed with her. When she saw Julie, the other woman stayed away from her. Holly wasn't stupid. Julie was planning something.

"Yeah, it's going to be fun." Mary stepped back, tucking some hair that had fallen out of her ponytail.

They were making progress on Holly's wedding. The appointment for the dress had been booked in the city. Holly already knew what dress she wanted. She had a good image inside her head. She only hoped the design was already available. There was no way she was waiting for a dress to be made to become Duke's woman in every sense of the word.

"I've got no chance of winning. There's no way vegetables win out over chocolate," Holly said, chuckling.

They both headed out of the diner to soak up the last of the sun. After today, Holly had seen the forecast wasn't good. Cold weather was making its way toward them with no sign of it disappearing.

"Did you hear what happened to Phil?" Mary asked.

"No, what?" She'd been busy dealing with the wedding and hadn't the time to listen to gossip.

"He's been fired. Trisha, the woman who works on the main desks, said David called Phil into his office. There was a lot of shouting and the last thing David told Phil was to get the hell out of his office." Mary kept talking as they stood, basking in the sun. In the last couple of weeks, her friend looked healthier, better than she'd ever seen her.

"Do you believe that?"

"Yeah, I do. I always told you that I didn't like him. He was weird," Mary said.

As if talking about him had made him appear in the flesh, Phil walked up to her.

"Hey, Holly, can I talk to you a second?"

Holly frowned. It was strange seeing Phil without his uniform. "Erm, sure." She looked toward Mary who was shaking her head. "I'll be back in a moment."

She followed Phil away from Mary. "I've just heard that you were fired. Is that true?" she asked, stuffing her hands back into her pockets.

"Yeah, not exactly my finest moment." He stared at her jacket. "I see you've moved up in the world."

"If you're just here to insult me," Holly said, turning back to head back to her friend.

"Fuck," Phil said, yelling the word. "Don't take this personally."

The sound of screeching wheels filled her senses. Before she had a chance to react, Phil slammed his fist into her face.

Everything went dark.

****

Duke pulled up at the diner, anticipation filling him. Holly had left his bed that morning, making her way into town toward Mary before he got a chance to fuck her. He wondered how she'd feel about fucking outdoors, up against a wall. His cock was rock hard, begging for her. It had been hard to get through club shit thinking about his woman.

"Why did we agree to this?" Pike asked, coming to stand beside him.

"What's wrong with trying some cake?"

"Knowing my luck, Mary's laced hers with rat poison." Pike had told him the truth about what went down with Mary. He'd told Holly the truth. They'd gotten together, had sex, and Pike had warned Mary about what he liked in the bedroom. Mary hadn't liked it, and so there wasn't going to be anything between them. Duke knew there was more to the story, but he'd left it alone. There was no use in causing any kind of argument.

Holly had also backed down seeing as Mary was happier for being apart from Pike. They rounded the diner and all came to a stop. There was an ambulance and a group of men surrounded a woman on the ground. Mac was in the center, looking completely freaked out.

Walking close, Duke was shocked to see Mary on a stretcher.

"I'm sorry, only family allowed," the paramedic said, pushing Mac aside.

"What the fuck happened?" Duke asked.

"Don't you answer your fucking phone?" Mac advanced toward them. Duke glanced back to see Pike had gone pale.

"What the fuck happened?" Duke stepped forward, gripping Mac's shirt. They'd clearly missed something.

"We saw the whole fucking thing. Phil, he took Holly. Wanted to talk to her or something. Mary wasn't making any sense." The blood in Duke's veins ran cold. *Phil, Holly?* What the fuck had happened?

"Tell me from the fucking start."

"Phil hit Holly. He knocked her out, grabbed her at the same time a black fucking truck pulled up in front of them. Mary screamed her name, but no one stopped. They ran her over. Mary charged for the van but didn't move out of the way. They clipped her, knocking her down." Mac ran a hand over his face.

"They?"

"Phil and whoever was in the van. I don't know, Duke. Fuck, I've got to get to the hospital." Mac left them alone, going to his car.

Turning back to his boys, Duke saw the anger on all of their faces. Russ was holding on by a thread.

"Some fucking bastard has taken my daughter." Russ gritted his teeth.

"We'll get her back." He looked at Pike. His gaze was on Mac's disappearing car. "Pike, are you with me or with Mary?"

Pike turned tortured eyes to Duke. "I'm with you. She'll never forgive me if I don't get Holly back."

Nodding, Duke headed back to his bike just as his cell phone rang. Glancing down at the screen he saw it was Matthew. Cursing, he answered the call. "Son, I've not got time."

"Dad, Mom's fucked up. I mean really fucked up." It sounded like Matthew was holding back sobs. Duke tensed.

"What's going on?" he asked.

"Some guys came to the house. They were talking about you, Holly. Mom kept calling a guy dog. I don't know what it all means. They, Dad, they knocked me out. I think I'm in Mom's basement."

He was going to kill Dawg, and he was going to make sure Julie couldn't come near his boy again.

"Listen to me, Matthew, I'm sending one of the boys over to you. You hold on tight." After he reassured his son, he turned to Russ, letting the whole club know what was going on. "Will you get my boy?"

"Only if you get my girl."

He nodded, holding his hand out.

"Do you know where they are?" Pike asked, straddling his bike.

"No, but Diaz will know. Dawg's Crew has my girl." And his ex-wife had given her up. The bitch was going to go.

Chapter Fourteen

"We're waiting for Duke to pay for her. I don't give a fuck what you wanted. I want my money," Dawg said, yelling the words at Julie.

Holly watched the two go back and forth. Both were crazy. They'd taken her, and now they were arguing about what to do with her.

"She's a fucking whore."

"You're fucking crazy," Holly said, screaming at the entire room. She pressed a hand to her stinging cheek. Her head felt like it was going to explode. She was in so much pain, and it was all this bitch's fault. From the moment she'd woken up in the back of the truck, she'd been in a nightmare. She'd been restrained and on the floor. When the back of the truck opened up, they covered her eyes as they dragged her into this fucking place. The moment they removed the blindfold, she saw Julie, and she knew she was fucked. She couldn't believe Julie would be this fucking stupid.

"Shut up," Dawg said, glaring at her. "You told me she would give me a big fucking payday."

Julie smiled up at the large man. "She will. Duke will pay for the slut. You can use her as well. You can do whatever the hell you want with her."

"No, you can't," Holly said, knowing Julie wanted them to rape her. The evil look in Julie's eye couldn't be mistaken for anything else. She was so pissed off and scared. Julie was high on drugs, and her associates looked even more high.

Dawg had already hit her for shouting at him. He didn't like her yelling. Her lip was split, swollen, and hurting. When she got free, she wanted to kill Julie.

"You touch me and you've got no chance of surviving."

"Ignore her, Dawg. She doesn't know what she's talking about. I do. I know what I'm talking about. Take her out of the picture and Duke will come back to me. I'll give you all the money you want." Julie tried to purr, but Dawg shrugged her off.

"Get the fuck away from me. Your pussy is washed up and old."

Glancing around her, Holly glared at the floor.

Phil was on the floor, blood pooling from the gunshot wound. He'd tried to demand more money, blackmailing them with evidence he had on all of them. Holly's heart was racing. There was no way she was coming out of this alive, and her thoughts didn't improve when she stared at Phil. If he was dead, she didn't stand a chance. These men were unstable. Their eyes were glazed over from the drugs they'd taken.

Glancing to her left she saw another man snorting some white powder. What the hell had Julie gotten herself into? This entire kidnapping was half-assed, and not thought out.

"You should take her, Dawg. Duke wouldn't want her afterwards and you can use her in one of your clubs. She'd earn you a lot of money."

Dawg grabbed Julie around the throat. "Don't turn this into something personal. The only thing I'm interested in is money and this fucking deal."

"Deal?" Holly asked. "You're insane to have trusted her. Duke will never do a deal with you."

"Shut your fucking mouth." Dawg released Julie long enough to land another blow to her cheek. Holly saw stars as she stared at the cement floor. She didn't have a clue where she was. "If Duke wants to see your fat ass again, he'll do what I say."

Pressing a hand to her cheek, she glanced up in time to see Julie smirking down at her. She hated that woman.

"Where's Matthew?" Holly asked.

The smile left Julie's face.

"You put him in danger you'll be high on Duke's kill list. Even if he can't save me, you're dead anyway."

"Shut her up," Julie said.

Holly cried out as she was kicked in the stomach. Gripping her stomach, Holly fought the tears that threatened to spill over. Pain slammed throughout the whole of her body. She needed to fight to give Duke time to find her.

"Call him," Dawg said, glaring at Julie.

This was totally fucked up.

"What?" Julie asked, looking confused

"Call your old man. I want this deal done."

Looking up she saw Dawg had a gun pointed at her head. Closing her eyes, Holly thought about Duke, Matthew, Mary, her parents, the club, all the people she loved and wouldn't get the chance to say goodbye. She wouldn't get to walk down the aisle to the man she loved.

Holding in a sob, she thought about Duke. His warm touch when he held her, caressed her. She would think about him, and death would be welcome.

"You don't need to call me," Duke said. "I'm already here."

Opening her eyes, Holly cried out as bullets started flying. Someone threw their body over her, hiding her.

"Stay still, Holly." Raoul growled the words into her ear, shielding her.

She didn't allow herself to think about what was happening. The club had come for her.

Minutes passed, which felt like hours. Finally Raoul pulled her to her feet. Looking around the room, she saw all of Dawg's Crew was dead. Pike was nursing an injury to his arm. What made her pause was the gun Duke had pointed at Julie's head.

****

Duke stared at the woman who gave birth to his son. He was waiting for one thing and then this woman would be out of his life forever. She didn't move as he had the gun pointed at her.

"Holly?"

Her hands wrapped around his waist. The scent of her surrounded him. Glancing down he saw the bruise on her face. They'd hurt her. Turning her head left and right, he looked into her eyes. "Are you okay, baby?"

"I'm fine." She smiled up at him. "You came for me."

"Always."

"So you fucking claimed her as your old lady," Julie said, sneering. "I should have known. You were always panting after her underage ass."

Come on, Russ.

His cell phone rang. He released Holly long enough to grab his phone and answer the call.

"Is he okay?"

"Yeah. He's got a couple of bruises. I'm taking him to the hospital."

"Good. Put him on."

"Dad?" Matthew asked seconds later.

"It's me."

"Dad, I don't want to ever see her again. I promise."

"Get to the hospital. I'll handle this shit." He disconnected the call and glared at Julie.

"I'm sorry, Duke," she said, sobbing.

He was unaffected by her tears. She'd put his woman in danger, hurt their son. Julie had used up all of her chances. He'd warned her, but she hadn't listened.

"Would you really kill the mother of your son?" she asked. "I'll get better. I'll be better."

"You're right. I couldn't kill the mother of my son, but I could kill the woman who put my family and the club in danger." Without any remorse at all, Duke fired his gun. Julie fell to the floor with a single bullet hole through her forehead.

Holly turned her head against his cut.

"Can we go?"

"Yes." Taking the lead, he made his way out of the warehouse, ordering his men to clean the shit up. "We've got to go to the hospital."

"Why?"

"Mary was run over. Your father's taking my son there as well." He cupped her cheeks, forcing her to look up at him. "I love you, Holly."

"I love you, too."

"I'm so sor—"

She stopped him from talking, pressing a finger to his lips. "No, you don't need to say sorry to me. You weren't the one responsible for Julie or Phil."

He'd seen greed had killed Phil. Taking her hand, they headed toward the hospital with Pike following close behind them. Holly held onto his waist. When they climbed off the bike, he stopped her from entering.

"Why are you not freaking out on me?"

"Because they all deserved to be killed. I'm your old lady, Duke. I'm loyal to you and the club." She went on her toes and kissed his cheek.

He'd just fallen in love with his woman all over again. She truly was a beauty.

****

Two days later

Mary looked toward the door expecting to see Holly. Her friend was supposed to be picking her up to take her home. When she saw Pike, she froze. She'd not seen him since that night when he took her virginity and torn out her heart. She'd never be good enough for him. His warnings had been read loud and clear.

"I thought Holly was coming to get me." She was supposed to be staying at the ranch with Holly and Duke until her leg healed up. Besides a lot of bruising, her broken leg was all that remained from her trying to get Holly from the truck.

"She's coming."

"What are you doing here?" The sound of his voice broke her heart. She could pretend for so long that she wasn't hurting, but the moment Pike entered her life, the pain returned. She was broken inside. There was no way to mend the pain. She'd tried. Mac had promised to take care of her while her leg healed up. She denied him. Mary didn't want to lead the other man on. She wasn't dating anyone.

"I wanted to come and see you, make sure you were okay."

"I'm fine."

"I don't want anything to be weird between us, Mary. Duke and Holly, they're getting married. She's his old lady. You're going to be around the club because of her."

"Do you want me to stop being her friend?" Mary asked. She wouldn't do it, not even for Pike.

"No."

"Good." She stared down at her bag. The pain medication she'd been given could only do so much to dull the ache in her leg. There was no medication to numb the pain in her heart.

"I need you to know what I did was for your own good."

Closing her eyes, she counted to ten in the hope he'd be gone. He wasn't. Pike moved closer to her. Didn't he know he was tearing her heart out and stamping on it?

"Please," she said.

He stroked the back of her neck. His touch only acted as a reminder to what he had done to her all those weeks ago.

"Mary?"

Pulling out of his touch, she grabbed the crutches, placing them underneath her arms. "You don't get to touch me, remember. I'm not old lady material, and the only thing you'd want me for was a cunt to lose yourself in. You can't be faithful to me. Leave me alone, Pike. I don't want anything to do with you."

Before he could say anything more Holly appeared in the doorway. She pasted a smile on her face, turning her back on Pike. If only she could turn her heart on him so easily.

Epilogue

The rumor mill went riot over Phil's actions that day. No one found a body, and to everyone's surprise, Dawg's Crew disappeared. Trojans MC wasn't even suspected of being involved. Holly told people who asked that she was able to sneak out of the truck when it had come to a stop. She'd kept up with her story. David, the Sheriff, was looking for another man to take Phil's place. Not many people were applying for the position.

Holly got her Christmas wedding inside the club. Mary was her maid of honor while Pike became Duke's best man. When it came to the dance, Mary looked like she wanted to knee Pike in the balls. With her leg still in a cast, the men who danced with her held her close so that she could join in the fun as well. Duke held his woman, taking her for the dance, and when night came, he carried her over the threshold of their ranch. They were still putting the finishing touches to the ranch with Matthew's help.

What did touch Duke was when Matthew asked for Holly to adopt him, becoming his stepmom. Duke didn't have a problem. He'd willingly share everything he was with his woman.

They saw the New Year in together at the club. Everyone was on their best behavior as Matthew and a couple of other kids were present. Duke sat on the wall near his bike with his woman in his arms. The love he felt for her was hard for him to control. He didn't think it was possible to fall more and more in love with her. He'd been mistaken. Holly owned his heart, body, mind, and soul. She held control over every part of him, but he held the same control over her.

"Duke," she said, shouting over the fireworks exploding in the sky.

"What, baby?"

She tilted her head back to smile at him. "I'm pregnant."

He froze, staring down at her.

"You're pregnant?"

"Yes." She put his hand over her stomach. "I forgot to go for the booster shot on the pill. I'm pregnant."

In answer, he cupped her cheek, kissing her until they were both breathless.

"Are you happy?" she asked.

"More than you can know."

He held a treasure in his arms. Unlike a lot of men who allowed their treasure to get away, he was going to keep Holly with him. She was his soul mate, the other half of him.

The End

www.samcrescent.wordpress.com

Evernight Publishing

www.evernightpublishing.com

14742615R00095

Printed in Great Britain
by Amazon.co.uk, Ltd.,
Marston Gate.